RICK THE DEAD CREOLE CLUB

Diana Marie DuBois

COPYRIGHT

Copyright © by Diana Marie DuBois 2025
All rights reserved. No part of this book may be reproduced or transmitted in any form or by any means electronic or mechanical. This includes photocopying, recording or by any information storage or retrieval system, without the express permission of the author, Diana Marie Dubois, www.dianamariedubois.com, except for use in reviews. This is a work of fiction. Names, characters, and places are either the creation of the author's imagination or are used in a fictitious way, and any resemblance to actual persons, living or dead, establishments, events or locales is purely coincidental.

Published by Three Danes Publishing L.L.C.

Cover art by Anya Kelleye www.anyakelleye.com
Cover Model: Nick Perkins
Photographer: Summer
Edited by Em Edits
Edited by Partners in Crime book Services
Formatted by EmCat Designs

RICK THE DEAD CREOLE CLUB

Diana Marie DuBois

Acknowledgments

To Summer for taking the most amazing photos and being there when I needed information on Elvis.

Nick Perkins for letting me use you as my muse.

Dedicated to Nick Perkins

"When things go wrong, don't go with them."
Elvis Presley

NOTE TO READERS

Dear Readers

If you are an Elvis fan you know that he was very spiritual as are the Elvis tributes that I have met. This book I decided to play on that bit somewhat more. There is a deep conversation between Baron Samedi and Elvis. I figured if he may have had a chance to speak to him this would have happened. Enjoy!

GLOSSARY

A little Less Sugar—Coffee shop owned by Madsion Watson friend to all the ETA's.
Baron Samedi—loa of the dead, resides in the underworld. Also, seventh gate keeper in the underworld.
Baron Kriminel—keeper of second gate of the Underworld. Also thought to be the first murderer and to have murdered Guede Nibo.
Bayou of lost souls—my made-up version of the River Styx.
Blue Moon Gallery—onced owned by the now dead Hyla Beachy now owned by Summer.
Blue Suede Bling—Elvis Clothing store owned by Stephen and managed by Ashley.
Clambake restaurant—managed by Melissa Ray
Cypress knees—roots of a cypress tree coming out of a swamp.
Dead Creole Club—Club owned by DB King, where the ETA's perform.
Elek Tavaloris—president of the Beast of Atonement Motorcycle club from that series.
Erzulie Freda--the vain and flirty goddess of love.

GLOSSARY

ETA's—Elvis Tribute Artists
Flaming Star—Club owned by Kingston Dupe.
Guede Nibo—the keeper of the second gate of the underworld.
Lawdy Lawdy Miss Clawdy—The hair salon owned by Heidi, friend to all ETA's.
Maman Bridgitte—Baron Samedi's wife.
Papa Legba—a loa who serves as the go-between for loas and humanity. You'll go to him at the crossroads.
Shake, Pinch & Roll—Bakery owned by Larisa Landry friend to all the ETA's and Aaron's g/f.
Stone Dragon—Motorcycle club in Beast of Atonement Series.
Veve—a religious symbol used in different branches of voodoo. They serve as a representation of the loa.
Voodoo—religion based on African worship. Not evil.

Song List for the Dead Creole Album

1. "King of the Dead" written by Diana Marie DuBois
2. "It's All Because of You" written by Cynthia Lucas
3. "An Evil-Hearted Woman" written by Diana Marie DuBois
4. "When I Rumble" written by Cynthia Lucas
5. "Voodoo Land Rock" written by Diana Marie DuBois
6. "Not That I Know Of" written by Diana Marie DuBois
7. "Voodoo Doll" written by Diana Marie DuBois
8. "Goodnight Mr. Langoustine" written by Cynthia Lucas
9. "Nightmare" written by Diana Marie DuBois
10. "Now, Forever and Always" written by Cynthia Lucas
11. "Underworld" written by Diana Marie DuBois
12. "Samedi" written by Diana Marie DuBois

INTRODUCTION

Baron Samedi

I sat behind my desk with my feet propped up, fiddling with an unlit cigar between my thumb and forefinger, when I heard a knock on the door.

"I wonder who that could be?" Skeley said, not bothering to glance up from the newest book he was reading.

I knew it wasn't Erik. He was off with Lawson searching for

Selvis and hadn't messaged me on this gadget. I looked down where it lay on the wooden desk.

Ignoring Skeley, I waved the door open a smidge, letting whoever was on the other side come in. But when no one entered, I ordered, "Come in."

The door opened wider, and Elvis peered around it. "Are you busy, Baron Samedi?"

I sat up, sliding my long, bony legs off the desk. My black pants got caught on an exposed nail, tearing the cuff just a tad. I tugged on them and shifted them back down over my alabaster bones before speaking. "No, come on in." I waved to him with my hand not holding my cigar.

"Good, I need to speak with you." He strutted around the door, and at that moment, I knew why all the girls screamed for him. It wasn't just his voice or his good looks. It was also his swagger; it was the way he moved his body. He glided as he walked. He exuded confidence, charm, and charisma even in death. This man was the whole package. He was dressed in a black suit with a high collar covering his neck, which was not his usual jumpsuit. He donned a red shirt with a short white scarf untied around his neck. One time, I heard that the other deity we don't speak of, when he made this man, broke the mold, and I began to believe this to be the truth.

"What is on your mind, Mr. Presley?"

He sat down, eyeing my cigar.

"Would you like one?" I waved mine at him."

The smile that etched across his handsome face reached all the way to his eyes, almost hypnotizing me. I had to shake free of his spell, but once again, I realized why the girls had screamed for him. This man was sex on a stick. Even I had to admit that. "I uh... I sure would." He stammered.

I stood up from my chair, my back to him, and opened the

fancy cigar box on a bookcase by the wall. Pulling another one out, I turned back to face him. I handed it to him along with the cutter. He put it in his mouth and cut the edge off. I leaned forward and lit it with my finger.

"How'd you do that?"

"It's part of being down here. The Underworld is full of possibilities." I grinned at him and then sat back down, leaning back in my chair. Propping my feet back on the desk.. Before I asked him again why he was there, I blew out little smoke skeletons and watched them dance around him. He watched in awe and smiled that beautiful smile of his. I had to be careful I didn't get sucked into his spell again, so I looked away.

"Baron Samedi, I am here because I have a question."

I puffed on my cigar. "Ask away," I responded, waving my free hand.

"Are you the Devil in Disguise?"

I laughed loudly. The sound reverberated off the walls. "No, I am not.

"Then what are your intentions with me and the tributes? Are they bad?"

My eyes went wide inside their bony orbits at this question. And I pulled my legs from the desk, placing them back on the floor, carefully avoiding the nail this time. My black boots scraped against the floor. Then I leaned forward again and steepled my fingers with the cigar hung haphazardly from the side of my mouth clenched between my teeth. "Mr. Presley, I am neither bad nor good." I pulled my steepled fingers apart, and placed them flatly on the desk. Removing the cigar from my mouth, I held it in my fingers and waved my hand around. "I am like that country Switzerland, you know, neutral."

"So then, why can we not mention God? He sat forward in his chair, puffing on his cigar. I could hear the sizzle of tobacco.

A slight scent found its way to my nonexistent nose. I leaned closer to him and sniffed. I'd never smelled anything like this on the dead before. What the hell? That aroma must be another reason the women found him so intoxicating. Upon further inspection, I took a closer look at the king of rock and roll. I could see the curve of his nose and how his sideburns framed his face. "What the hell is going on here?" I murmured to myself, then sucked in a breath clenching my teeth tightly. I chuckled as I pulled myself away from him. "You are a man of imminent faith, I presume?"

He nodded.

"We don't mention any other Gods here."

He looked at me in shock but did not utter a single word.

And I went back to my former position in my chair. "It is just that you humans like to mention him."

He nodded as if he was trying to make sense of things. "Then can I ask what is this place?"

I stood and walked around the desk, glad to finally describe my home to a visitor. Rarely did I get to have a tete-a-tete with someone of value. I had only had it with one other person, and he cannot be mentioned. I pulled myself out of my thoughts with a smile plastered across my face. "My boy, this is a place of grandeur." I danced around with my arms in the air, tipping my hat to the King of Rock and Roll. I replaced my hat and grinned at Elvis. "It is a form of limbo. When I take souls to the seventh gate, I send them where they are meant to go. I do not judge. That is not my job. I have no idea where they go. For all I know, they go to that place where your... Uh, your... Um..."

I heard a snort from over by the wall and glared at Skeley over Elvis's shoulder. I could see him mouthing the word God lives. I took my free hand and did a slicing motion across my neck, telling Skeley to stop his bad behavior, though I knew it wouldn't stop him.

"I have another question.

"You are full of questions today." I grimaced.

"Is it true then that you are a trickster?"

"Where did you hear that?" I tried hard to hold in my anger.

"Well, I've been hearing whispers around Guede Nibo's place that you're a sort of a trickster.

I chuckled loudly and heard Skeley snicker from his painting behind Elvis. I raised a brow. "And just who have you heard this from, may I ask?" Fear registered on his face, and he started to backtrack. "I...uh...don't...remember," he stuttered.

Knowing that I wouldn't get it out of him and I didn't want to scare him, I asked, "So, do you have any more questions for me?"

"Yes. What will you do once you're finished playing with all of us."

The cigar nearly fell from my mouth, but I quickly caught it before it caused any damage to my beloved little skeletons inside my desk. I tried to hide my apparent shock and anger at the question, but he just stared at me, a cigar pressed between his lips. "Mr. Presley, it would be wise not to anger me."

"Baron Samedi, I meant no disrespect. I just wanted to know if I can return to where you pulled me from. I was almost through the gates when..." he stopped speaking as I glared at him.

"That will be enough." I leaned back in my chair, propping my feet on my desk, and puffed on my cigar.

He looked sad for an instant. And for a little while, and no more than that, I felt a tinge of guilt. But it quickly dissipated.

So, all I could deduce was that his spell was also dissolving, which made me happy. "Baron Samedi, I was almost at the point where I was at peace. And that felt good for once."

I tried to hold my anger at bay. "Mr. Presley, I haven't decided yet. But I will say I can do anything with the snap of my fingers." I turned my alabaster head in his direction, blew a smoke skull in his way, and held up two of my fingers. "But you, my blessed King of Rock and Roll, will be the first to know when I decide on anything going on topside." I waved my hand and opened the veil. "Watch this," I told the singer.

His eyes went wide as the hazy movie of an apartment came into view. "What's going on?" He asked, knowing it was best to change the subject.

"Not sure, but let's watch and see. Hey, look, there's one of your precious tributes," I said, almost giddy. "He doesn't look so good. I wonder what's happened. I need to hear this."

I waved my hand, and suddenly, a stereo sound system played around us.

Where Could I Go But to the Lord
Rick

January 5th

My cell rang loudly, and I glanced at the number. "I wonder why they are calling me?" I said, glancing at the caller ID.

Who is it?" My only remaining roommate, Jacob, asked.

I ignored him and hesitantly answered the phone. But as the voice on the other end spoke, my body went numb, and I hit the yellow and green linoleum kitchen floor. My breath felt like it had been knocked out of me, and I could no longer breathe.

"Rick, what the hell is going on? You look as if you've seen a ghost." His voice sounded far away.

I couldn't speak. My voice wouldn't let me. It betrayed me. I dropped the phone and just knelt on the floor, unable to speak as my world collapsed with one phone call.

"Rick! Rick, what's wrong?" Jacob kept asking me, but I couldn't answer. I still couldn't utter a single word even though I was trying to speak. I kept opening and closing my mouth, willing myself to say the words, but every time I tried, nothing came out.

There was a numbness that wrapped itself around me. I couldn't shake it off, no matter how hard I tried. I vaguely saw Jacob pick up my phone, speak, and then hang up.

"I'm calling DB," Jacob said. His worried voice trailed off as he left me as a huddled mess on the floor to get his phone.

Fifteen minutes later

I barely heard the knock on the door from my bedroom as I sat in a chair staring out the window. I don't even remember getting to my room. I was just there.

"How's he doing?" I heard DB ask Jacob, I presumed from the living room.

"As good as can be expected considering the news he received."

"Where is he?"

"In his room."

The door creaked open, but I didn't move. The mattress groaned as DB sat down on the bed. He didn't speak at first. We just sat in silence for about ten minutes, but he finally asked, "Rick, what exactly did her parents tell you?"

Without turning around to look at him, I opened my mouth,

though my tongue stuck to the roof of my mouth like I'd just eaten a whole jar of peanut butter. I tried swallowing again to get some saliva to wet the inside of my mouth as if that would help the cotton mouth I had going on. Then I turned around in the chair. "Her," I choked back a sob, "Mother told me that her helicopter had gone down and that the army hadn't heard from her." That feeling in my chest started to come again, so I dropped my head between my knees. "I feel like I'm dying. I can't breathe." I gasped for air.

"Take it easy," DB told me. "Maybe everything will be all right. Not all is lost. You have to think positive."

"Maybe. But we hadn't been able to talk lately. She's been on maneuvers. She was supposed to come to visit, and I had planned on..." I paused. I couldn't say it out loud because now it would never happen.

"You planned to what?" DB prodded me to talk.

"I planned to propose to her." I choked out the confession.

With my back to him, I spoke. "DB, Josephine has to be fine. She must be."

DB stood and patted me on the shoulder. "Why don't you light a candle for her at St Louis Cathedral." His tone was comforting. "We have to stay positive during this time."

I looked up at him. "You know what? That's a good idea. I'll do that," I solemnly agreed as I glanced away.

I could hear DB moving toward the door. I moved in the chair and started to get up but stopped and stared at him. His smile was kind. "After you do that, try stopping at the club."

"I will try my best." I plastered on my best fake smile.

"Good."

After DB had gone, I sat there but remembered what he said. Maybe lighting a candle would do some good. I slowly stood, grabbed my keys off the nightstand, and trudged outside.

"Jacob, I'm going out to light a candle for Josephine," I hollered as I closed the door behind me.

I walked the distance to the huge church to say a prayer and speak to the big man about Josephine. The crowds at this time of day were thick, so I had to maneuver through them like a ship through the fog. Then there I was, staring at St. Louis Cathedral. For a second, I just took in the scenery and contemplated entering. I opened the wooden doors and entered. Off to my right was a vestibule with a dozen or so little red candle holders and candles. I took one of the long sticks, lit it, and said a silent prayer for Josephine.

Please, *dear God, bring Josephine back home to me safe and sound.*
Amen

Then, I did the sign of the cross.

After lighting the candle and saying my prayer, I stuffed a donation into the box in front of the candles and left, hoping that God was listening.

A few tourists walked past me as I left the vestibule, but I couldn't leave the church just yet. So, I opened the big wooden doors and stepped inside. Sitting in the farthest wooden pew, I kept silent and contemplated why I was there. I hoped God would hear my prayers and answer them. I remained quiet as I let the sanctity of the place just wash over me.

Finally, I decided to leave. When I stepped outside, darkness shrouded the sky. I glanced at my watch and realized I had about thirty minutes to get to the club, but did I really want to go?

Chorus
Baron Samedi

As the veil remained open, I wondered out loud. "It always baffled me that the humans went to church to ask God for help with things that troubled them."

"Maybe they feel like that's the only place they can go for help," Elvis told me as he puffed on his cigar.

"The loas could help them as well. There were those in the city who called on us for help with such matters."

I leaned back in my purple wingback chair and huffed. "Some can go to the humans to help, like the lovely Erzulie Freda. We just request an offering."

Elvis raised an eyebrow at me. "You see, God doesn't require an offering. We can speak to him any time we like, anywhere we like."

"Yes, but does God always answer you?" I replied. "Will your lovely tribute get the answer he expects?" I cocked my head at Elvis.

"God is always there but he doesn't always give you the answer you expect." Elvis answered. "As for what will happen with the tribute, that I don't know. That is for God to answer."

I realized at that moment, while having a tit for tat with the King of Rock and Roll, that he was smarter than the average human gave him credit for. To them, he was a common hillbilly. I could talk to this man for hours and hours, but I did not want him to know that. It was going to be my secret and my secret alone. The more I got to know him, the more I saw the reason people were drawn to him.

"Where is Erik, Skeley?" I asked the painting on the wall, quickly changing the subject, not wanting Elvis to think I was enjoying our conversation.

"I think he is with Lawson. They are out looking for Selvis," Skeley said from his post on the wall. "Don't you remember?"

"I do, but I thought he would have been back by now."

Elvis sat in the chair and puffed on his cigar. "You... uh... still haven't found my other half?" I noted a smidge of concern in his voice, but he tried hard to hide it.

"No, and I am getting rather worried."

"To be honest, so am I." Elvis leaned back, stretching his long lean legs in front of him. "What is going to happen if we don't find him?"

"That, my dear boy, is the million-dollar question."

I knew the answer, but was not ready to tell the King of Rock and Roll.

Thinking About You
Rick

Once I arrived at the club, Robert met me at the door. "Hey Rick, they're waiting for you."

I paused, hesitant to go inside. "Are they?"

He put a big hand on my shoulder as I stood just beyond the threshold debating about going inside. "Sorry to hear about your girlfriend."

"Thanks, man. How'd you hear about it?" I asked.

"Don't you worry about that. Just keep your thoughts positive," he told me, still holding the door open.

"Trying my best." I nodded weakly, deciding to finally go inside.

He changed the subject. "Are you going to be performing tonight?"

"I'm going to put forth my best effort," I said, suddenly stopping in the doorway.

"What's wrong?" He asked.

"Not sure. Suddenly, I don't feel like performing.

"Well, that is sort of a conundrum, isn't it? But maybe your girlfriend wouldn't want you stop doing what you love." He arched a brow at me.

I nodded. "Perhaps," is all I said as I crossed the threshold of the club.

"I hope you get it sorted it out." He patted me on the shoulder. "Anyway, I see we have a good crowd assembling tonight." He closed the door behind me, and I sauntered toward the dressing room, hoping I had time to get dressed.

"Damn, Robert was right. This place sure is packed."

I scanned the front tables as I passed, and saw some of our regulars. Rose and Frankie were there with Tina, Sandra, Andrea and Arlene behind them. Up close to the stage was Summer with her camera. I sure hoped she was able to get some good shots. There was a young girl with her who I'd never seen before. Maybe I'd ask DB who she was.

Larisa, Kiera, and Maddie waved at me from their usual table. I assumed, from the expressions on their faces, they were missing Hyla and Elodi. I made a mental note to talk to them after the show and check on them.

Then, I noticed Heidi walking to the bar with two drinks. She was followed by Bre, one of the bartenders, who brought more drinks. That was good. She was a good one for lifting someone's spirits.

I smiled and continued down the hallway to the dressing rooms. Aaron was sitting at one of the stations.

"Hey man, did you see all the people out there?" I pointed past the door. "We are going to have one hell of a night."

He turned around and grinned. "Sure, did. Though it's a shame we're missing some of our regulars." he sighed.

"Yes, such a shame. But I saw Heidi was hanging out with Larisa and Madison," I said, sitting down at my station.

"That's good. Heidi needs that as much as they do. It will be good for all involved," Aaron said as he glanced in the mirror to make sure everything was fine.

"So, no one's heard from Elodi?" I asked, turning around in my chair.

He shook his head. "Nope. Larisa is beside herself, but she did get a goodbye note from her."

"She did? Did she say where she was going?" I asked curiously.

He turned, but gazed into the corner of the room as if seeing something or someone before answering me. "No, she didn't. She just said she needed to get away from here. I guess being kidnapped took a toll on her. The sad thing is, she doesn't know what happened to Robin."

DB peeked into the room, interrupting us. "Fifteen minutes until showtime guys. Jacob's already waiting to go on stage. So, I need you two to hurry up."

"Yes, boss man," we said in unison.

Aaron stood and came over to me. "You ready? I know you are going through a tough time right now. Maybe performing is what Josephine would want you to do."

I laughed, remembering Robert saying almost the same thing when I came into the club.

I nodded. "Just give me a few more minutes."

"Sure," he said, grabbing a few dozen scarves and heading out. The music could be heard as he opened the door, but it became muffled the second it closed.

I sat there thinking of Josephine and that's when a memory

played in my head like a movie reel clicking over and over until it stopped on one scene.

One day, before I had a performance in the Union Halle in Bad Nauheim, I decided to take a walk. I found myself meandering along the pedestrian bridge where the people of the small town had erected a bronze statue in honor of Elvis.

Standing on the bridge, taking photographs in front of it, was the most breathtaking girl I'd ever seen. She was with a group of other girls, but I didn't pay the others any attention. It was her who caught my eye.

She had long black hair and the most beautiful sparkling blue eyes. I was mesmerized by her beauty. Her smile and her laugh were contagious. I stood gazing at her and barely heard my friend, Zerrin, who was in Germany performing with me. He walked up and nudged me on the shoulder. "Rick, Rick. Hey, earth to Rick.

I didn't want to pull my gaze from the girl who was laughing and smiling in front of me. When I didn't answer, he stepped in front of me, blocking my view of her. "Hey Rick, you ready to get a bite to eat before tonight's performance."

I tried to see around him but, in that instant, she had disappeared into the crowd.

"Who are you staring at?" He turned around to follow my gaze.

But I couldn't answer him. I was totally tongue tied. I just stood there staring into the crowd, scanning it, searching for her. The beautiful girl with the long black hair was gone.

And just like that, the memory died. I blinked, coming back to the here and now. The door to the dressing room opened and the music blared. I wondered who might have opened it, so I decided to investigate, but no one appeared.

Hurrying, I picked out one of my many jumpsuits. The joke was that I was addicted to them, so I had plenty to pick from. Once I had made my choice I quickly got dressed. Maybe I still had time to do a song or two. I had to get up and go perform, if not for me, for Josephine.

Forty minutes later

I stared into the mirror and grinned back at myself. Maybe not my best, but since I was strapped for time and didn't want to miss the show, it was what I had to work with. Hopefully, the audience wouldn't notice it was a rush job instead of my usual hour to hour and forty minutes of perfection.

I stood, did one more look in the mirror, grabbed some scarves, and headed out. I walked solemnly through the hallway leading to the stage. I heard the audience cheering loudly and knew the show was probably nearly halfway over. Just as I made my way up the back steps, Jacob ran off the stage. His smile was bigger than I'd ever seen.

"Did you see my performance?"

"I did." I lied. "Great job.," I said, smoothing down the pants on my jumpsuit, not daring to look him in the eyes.

"It's nice of you to finally join us," Aaron joked, standing backstage.

Thankfully, Jacob didn't hear him. He was still on his high from the cheers from the audience.

I nodded. "Have you been on?" I asked.

"Yes. We were waiting for you. Hoping you were going to

perform tonight, and here you are." He nodded to DB, who stepped backward a little on the stage, looking in our direction.

I smiled at him. He returned the gesture then turned back to the crowd.

DB KING GAVE the audience what they desperately craved, the ever-popular joke.

"What do you call an angry carrot? A steamed vegetable." The audience erupted into loud and ruckus laughter. "Yes, ladies and gentlemen, I'll have many more jokes to sport tonight as well as more jackets." DB strutted across the stage in his silver jacket as he talked into the microphone. "Now, are you finally ready for our next performer?"

They screamed and went wild.

"I thought so." He smiled, looking at us in the wings. "Without further ado, let me introduce our next performer, Mr. Rick Miceli, performing Thinking About You."

The crowd erupted in thunderous applause. DB left the stage and handed me the mic. "Thanks," I said, accepting it and walking onto the stage. "Hello, ladies and gentlemen. Are you having a good night tonight?"

Again, the crowd erupted with cheers.

"Good. This song is for someone special to me. I hope you like it." I turned to The Dead Creole band and the Dead Inspirations behind me. "Let's do this." They nodded and followed my lead.

The tune started out soft and slow. I let the words flow like butter. I held the mic in my right hand and felt the words to the bottom of my heart. The audience became mesmerized by the words, singing along with me. I gave the song everything I had as I swayed in sync with the sultry music.

The lyrics hit home at the thought I might have lost Josephine, but I wasn't going to let it get the better of me. I continued to belt it out, shaking my right leg slowly in sync with the music, then raising my hand in perfect Elvis fashion at the crescendo of the song.

Once the song was over, there wasn't a dry eye in the club. The audience wiped their faces with napkins or the ever-present scarf. I knew Josephine would be proud of me. But I also knew I couldn't do another song without getting news about her whereabouts. Walking off the stage, I handed the mic back to DB.

He started to speak, but I interrupted him. "I need to go see if Josephine's parents have called me."

He nodded in understanding. As I left backstage, Jess Wade passed me. I heard DB introducing him. I headed to the dressing room where I left my cell, but when I checked it, there were no missed calls.

Devastation was an understatement as I glanced at my phone. Then something fell in the back of the dressing room, pulling me away from my phone. Placing it on one of the tables, I went in search of the noise.

"Who's here?" I called out but was answered with silence.

I continued to walk around the dressing room but still found no one. An eerie and cold sensation, as if someone was in the room with me, crawled up my back. After a thorough search, I decided to leave and go check out the rest of the performances.

Just as I stepped outside, VK was going on stage. I headed toward the bar where the others sat. After a few moments, Heidi came up and patted me on the shoulder. "Hey guys. Do you remember Courtney?"."

I spoke up first. "Sure, it's been a while." Pausing, I tried to remember where her mother, Tina said she'd been studying. "Haven't you been in England?" I suddenly remembered.

Her eyes lit up and continued upward to her mouth. "You remembered?"

"Did you meet any ETA's while you were out there?" I asked curiously.

She smiled. "Yes, I met a few. I became good friends with Louis Brown."

Jacob pushed his way to the bar. "Hey, I don't think I've been introduced?" Jacob held his hand out to the tall brunette.

"Oh, sorry, about that," Heidi quickly apologized. "Jacob, this is my friend, Courtney. Courtney, this is Jacob Ray. You've probably seen her mom and grandmother down in the front row. Courtney is visiting from England," Heidi told him, smiling big.

"What were you doing all the way across the ocean?" Jacob asked, chugging back his drink.

"Studying."

"What were you studying?" I interrupted asking.

She blushed. "I'm almost done with a degree in Arts and humanities at Cambridge.

"Wow!" Jacob exclaimed.

LARISSA KIERA, and Madison came up to the bar noticing Courtney. They all took turns hugging her. "When did you get back home?" Larissa asked.

"Yesterday." She didn't blink an eye at Larissa being in a chair.

"My mom told me about Hyla and Elodie. I'm so sorry." She said sadly.

"Yes but we are taking it day by day." Kiera spoke up.

Courtney quickly changed the subject. "Hey, if you know of anyone with a job opening, I'm looking for something while I'm visiting," Courtney sweetly said.

"I could always use someone at the coffee shop," Madson offered.

"Seriously? That would be great." She grinned widely.

Wishing that Josephine was here to hang out with these girls, I suddenly changed the subject to take my mind off her. "Heidi, how's the salon doing?"

Before she answered, I saw sadness creep into her expression, but it disappeared as quickly as it appeared. "It's going just great. I just wish my dad was..." She stopped and sucked in a breath.

I placed a hand on her shoulder. "No need to finish that sentence. He knows. And he's so proud of you."

"I know." She went to wipe a tear that dared to slide down her cheek, but I beat her to it and wiped it from her face with my thumb. "It's so hard sometimes," she said.

"Just know that all of us are here for you anytime," I told her, looking around at everyone standing at the bar.

All the girls agreed in unison as they placed comforting hands on her shoulder.

"I know, and thank you for that."

From my peripheral vision, I saw something so I turned around. However, when I focused on it, I saw nothing.

"What the hell?" I wondered loudly.

Heidi smiled at me suspiciously causing me to laugh.

"Don't worry, I think we have ghosts in the club." Suddenly, I remembered that Robin was probably somewhere, and he was who was in the dressing room causing all the racket.

DB came up to the bar. "Hey girls, we are closing."

"It's all right, we need to leave anyway. Six am comes early, you know," Madison said, putting her glass down on the bar as she glanced at Larisa and Kiera.

"Yeah, we have to go, too," both girls said, looking at Madison. "Isn't that correct?"

"Yes," they agreed with her.

"Tell Aaron I'll see him later," Larisa told DB.

"Oh no you won't." Aaron came running from the back. "DB, I'll see you tomorrow. I'm going to make sure the girls get home safe and sound."

DB nodded and watched as they left.

The phone rang behind the bar and Betty answered it. "Yes, he's here. Hold on. It's for you, Rick," she said, covering the mouthpiece.

I stepped forward and took the receiver. "Hello, this is Rick."

I didn't hear the whole conversation as I went numb. My heart plummeted and there was a sickening feeling in the pit of my stomach. I tried my best to hold the urge to vomit at bay. This couldn't be happening. The phone slid from my hand and bounced against the bar. I felt the air sucked out of me as this time my whole world fell apart for real.

Chorus
Baron Samedi

Elvis and I sat there contemplating what would happen if we never found Selvis. I think we both secretly knew what would happen. Deep down, I knew, but did not want to say it out loud. After all, I was the reason he was in this predicament.

I knew it scared the crap out of him. I needed to get these two back together, or I feared they would cease to exist. I could feel it and if I could, I knew Elvis and his other half could as well. It was my fault, but I was not about to admit it to anyone.

Elvis suddenly pulled me from my thoughts. "Baron Samedi, I think Selvis knows something's wrong."

I glanced at him, knowing my assumptions were about to be proven correct. "What makes you say that?"

He hesitated slightly before speaking.

I tried prodding him, even though I knew it could be quite

dangerous to discuss. "Why do you say that?" I cautiously inquired, looking around then leaning forward. "Be careful. We seem to have spies lurking around," I whispered looking around.

He faltered again. I wondered what caused his hesitation. Maybe he did not trust me enough to discuss it with me. Who could blame him? I needed to change the situation.

I decided to coax him into telling me how he knew what was happening. "Elvis, tell me why you think Selvis knows something is wrong." I was also curious about when he last saw him.

His eyes went wide. Then he sighed, ultimately relenting.

Groaning, he leaned back in his chair then spoke. "Because, whenever he finds a tribute, he gives them an item of mine. Then, he touches them." Elvis paused, and I wondered if he was debating about telling me the rest. Then he continued. "He'd say darn it didn't work. It was if he thought if he touched the tribute, we would be one again."

I tapped my chin. "Very interesting, indeed. When was the last time you saw him?" I inquired, hoping it would give me insight I could pass onto Erik and Lawson.

"When he gave Robin…" He stopped, and I assumed he was afraid to give me too much information about what he'd been up to with the tributes.

I chuckled low in my throat and placed my palms flat on the desk. "Elvis, I know Robin's been leaving the club at night because of the necklace Selvis gave him and…" I hesitated then chuckled low in my throat. "…may I add, I also know about you leaving a little piece of you in each of the tributes when you leave them."

He gasped loudly. "Why haven't you said anything?"

"Robin leaving the club was in the fine print of his contract," I guffawed. I foresaw it so wrote it in there.

"Uh...seriously? How did you know about me leaving parts of me when I left them?"

"It was bound to happen. When a soul inhabits another body, it is just something that can occur." I replied, solemnly leaning back into my chair and settling my long legs out in front of me on the floor. My tone took on a serious tone. "But remember, as I told you before, we must be careful when speaking of him and your suspicions. You could get caught in a trap."

"You're right." His thoughts seemed to drift off.

"You know, you might want to get back to Guede Nibo before he starts looking for you or others find you here. At least, at his gate, you are somewhat protected."

He chuckled. "You mean, I'm not protected at the great and powerful Samedi's?" He raised his hands in the air in fascination.

"It is not that." I started to backtrack my faux pas. In fact, I did not want my wife to see him. Elvis was mine. However, I never answered his question. "I will send you back with a snap of my fingers, so you don't have to worry about anything." Rubbing my thumb and forefinger together, the King of Rock and Roll disappeared from my office.

"Boss man, what are you going to do if you don't find his other half?" Skeley inquired from his painting on the wall.

"I have no idea right now. But we need to find Selvis, or at least, get them in close proximity to one another."

Skeley gasped loudly, slamming down his book. The echo caused his painting to rattle on the wall.

"What's wrong, Skeley?" I asked, panic evident in my tone.

"Shh. Someone's here."

"Are you sure?"

"Yes, I can feel him."

"Who?"

"I don't know. But there's someone in the room with us."

Suddenly, I walked over to the corner of the room and stared. I blinked my eyes as I saw something hazy. Whatever I thought I saw, or didn't see, disappeared in an instant.

Interlude

I hid deep in the shadows of Baron Samedi's office, as was my nature, and eavesdropped on the two. I was careful to remain still as not to be heard or seen. I knew the magic painting was able to sense me.

My benefactor would be impressed with what I'd found out. If this information was true, it was imperative that I find the one they called Selvis before the bone man and his entourage found him.

I sensed he was up to something. I'd had him once before, but he'd managed to escape. This time, I would make sure he remained just where I put him. Flipping open my trusty timepiece, I checked the time then closed it with a click. But the noise of my watch must have alerted the one they called Skeley that I was in the room. Because the man with the top hat peered right at me in my hiding spot. It was a good thing I could no longer breath because he would be able to hear my breaths coming out in panics. As he stared at me I remained still and sucked myself even further into the shadows.

Before I got caught, I shimmered out of the room.

I Wish the World Would Go Away
Rick

Two days later

After I received the devastating phone call, I sat at the bar wishing the world would disappear and take me with it. My world crumbled around me, and I didn't know how to make it stop. Instead of doing as I wished, I was left to drink everything away with liquor.

"Hey Betty, can I get another Kentucky Bourbon Rain?" I slid the glass her way. It almost crashed to the floor, but she caught it as it went over the edge of the bar.

"Good catch."

I heard a familiar voice. My head spun around. I faced a longtime friend I hadn't seen since he'd taken over another club on the Northshore.

"Well, it lookshh like the prodigal..."

Betty slid me another glass. I grabbed it and slugged the brown liquid down my throat. It burned, but I didn't care. Slamming the glass down on the bar, I looked at our new guest.

"...shon has returneddd. Weee...misshhhed youuu... sho much." My slurring tone became sarcastic with the last bit of alcohol.

"You look like you're not doing so well." He smirked.

"Well, youuu... like you sheeem to be doinggg better...." Continuing to slur, I reached out to shake his hand. Missing slightly, I almost toppled off the barstool.

Chuckling, he caught me under my arms before I face-planted. "It looks like I'm doing better then you."

DB came from the back but stopped as he saw Kingston help me from falling off the barstool. The glare he cast toward us was not lost on me, even though I was drunk.

Quickly recovering, DB walked over and mockingly greeted Kingston. "Don't mind him. He received some bad news a couple of days ago, so he's been drinking away his sorrows."

"Seriously."

He peered over at me, but I was too busy ignoring him as I stared into the glass Betty had refilled. I watched the little ice cubes dance among the brown liquid, but all I saw were memories of a dead girlfriend floating among the ice cubes in my glass. It was as if they were tiny icebergs telling me I would be alone forever. I so badly wanted to smash them to pieces.

I tried to ignore the two men as they talked. I just wanted to continue to drown my sorrows, but DB was right beside me.

"So, what brings the elusive Kingston Dupe to my club?" DB asked, leaning against the bar, a little too close for my liking, but that could have been the alcohol talking. Either way, I heard the suspicion in his question.

Glancing up, I saw the two men at what I could only deduce as a standoff. Kingston suddenly stuffed his hands into his pockets. "Well, speaking of clubs, that's what I came to talk to you about."

"What about it?" DB asked curiously with apprehension in

his voice "I thought you had the club business all thought out." His tone was sarcastic.

Sighing deeply, Kingston confided, "Well, it's not doing too well." He looked around. "I can say with unabashed certainty, it is not as good as yours."

"What happened? You couldn't handle things on your side of the lake?" DB's tone became increasingly alarming. I didn't blame him, especially after what happened between them.

I ignored them by asking Betty for another drink at the top of my lungs. "Betty, can I get another one."

Slamming my glass down on the bar, I almost broke it. DB glared at me, but then refocused on Kingston.

I badly wanted to tell him I wasn't the prodigal son, that Kingston was, so to stop glaring at me. Instead, I continued to nurse my drink, but not before I returned DB's glare.

He ignored me, so, I returned my focus to Betty who was wiping out a glass. Maybe if I smiled at her enough, she would stop disregarding me and I would win another Kentucky Bourbon Rain.

"DB..." Kingston paused, sighed, then continued, "...the Flaming Star is about to go under." Sighing softly, he continued. "My tributes have threatened to leave. I don't want them to. They are beyond talented."

"You should have thought about that before you did what you did." DB angrily replied.

Keeping my back to them, I cupped the glass in my hand. Pushing it around on the bar, I intently gazed at the swirling liquid. When I got bored, I focused on my surroundings.

From my peripheral vision, I watched Kingston as he removed his baseball hat then nervously rubbed his head. Nonchalantly replacing it, he refolded the bill. "Do you think you could help me?"

I almost fell off the barstool as I turned and laughed haughtily. "You have got to have the biggest balls I've ever seen—especially after what you did."

Kingston's expression softened. "You know Zerrin misses you and your friendship."

"You leave Zerrin out of this." I spat then turned around. Talking with my back to him. "He should be apologizing for his own shortcomings. And he passed on our friendship when he left with..." I stopped talking afraid I'd already said too much." I turned away, wishing I had ignored his comment about my old friend. Instead, I grew angry about other things. With my back to both men, I muttered, "Yeah, DB, why don't you help him? Maybe it's what they all deserve. Tell them what they are in for. What happens here." I spun around on the barstool and stared at him. "Tell him what happened to Aaron or Josh. Oh, where is Josh? Better yet, tell him what *you*..." I stressed the word, "...had to do to keep this club." I was screaming, but DB stood there calmly, staring. He wasn't angry. He was calm, and that made me even angrier. "Damn it, DB, tell Kingston what happens to the tributes when you help them."

DB turned to me. "First of all, I will never help Kingston. He lost my trust a long time ago." His expression remained stoic.

Kingston didn't flinch at the announcement, but after a few moments he finally spoke up. "You mean the deals with the bone man?"

My jaw dropped in shock. "So, you know already about him?" DB and I asked.

"I know he makes deals with many in the city. How do you think your club is doing so well, DB, yet mine is failing? I need help."

"Again, you should have thought about that and not done

what you did." DB was exasperated as he turned to me then to Kingston. "Can we discuss this later?"

I couldn't deal with it. I dropped my head on the bar. The alcohol was starting to wear off and I didn't want that. I wanted it to take a hold of me. I wanted to close my eyes. I wanted everyone to leave. I wanted everyone to leave me alone.

DB remained by my side. He placed a hand on my shoulder, I'm sure it was meant to comfort me, but I was in no mood for it. I wanted to be left alone.

I desperately thought about shoving his hand off me, then decided against it. Instead, I just thought about Josephine and closed my eyes. I overheard DB talking to Kingston. His tone made me wonder if there was more to what had happened between them. More than what I knew.

"I'll decide on your tributes later. I think we have more pressing matters to discuss." His tone turned to disgust.

My eyes slowly popped open because that was all I could muster. I shrugged DB's hand from my shoulder. "You are talking about me, aren't you?" With difficulty I dragged my head up from the bar and glared at him. "Am I the more pressing matter?" I pointed a finger at my chest then shook my head emphatically. "No, I'm just sitting here drinking and enjoying myself. Hey Betty, I need another drink," I said as I tried to get her attention. She ignored me. I faced DB and glared. "Look, what do you want me to do?"

"I want you to grieve, but not this way." DB's expression was sad. I didn't know what to do with his sadness.

After a few minutes of concentrating on it, I grew angry. "So, what if I'm drowning my sorrows in this wonderful bourbon."

I shook my glass, letting the almost melted ice clink softly. I hoped Betty got the hint to refill it, but her back was to me. She was still ignoring me. On further inspection, I saw that she was talking to someone. But it couldn't be. There was no one there. Maybe I was extra drunk. I shook my head and dismissed my craziness.

DB replaced his hand on my shoulder. "I want you to deal with your grief, but drinking is not the way to handle it."

I roughly shrugged his hand off my shoulder. "I am dealing with it," I said through gritted teeth. "I am drinking it away."

"What happened?" Kingston asked, his voice full of concern.

"I don't know if it's any of your business, Kingston," DB retorted.

"Well, if you must know..." I turned to Kingston. "...I found out that Josephine, my girlfriend, was killed in a helicopter crash in Germany where she was stationed. Why don't you run back and tell my so-called best friend, Zerrin, that and see what he does with that piece of news," I said, irked.

"Don't be like that." Kingston looked sorry for once.

I turned my back on him and willed Betty to give me another drink. "Betty... oh, Betty... Damn it, Betty can I get another drink?" She continued to ignore me. I assumed DB had secretly told her to cut me off. All I could do was sit there, mope, and feel sorry for myself.

"Kingston, you're going to have to come back later. I have more pressing things at hand," DB said, none too happy.

"DB, if you are going to talk about me like a child, I'll be leaving."

He stopped his conversation with Kingston. "Rick, no, you're drunk. You will not be driving.

"I hadn't planned on driving home since I didn't drive here," I said sarcastically.

Without missing a beat, DB leaned against the bar. "I'll get

Aaron to take you home. Tomorrow, I'll call Josphine's parents and check on the funeral."

"Fine," I grumbled, slamming the glass on the bar, causing it to shatter. Glass littered the bar and trickled down to the floor.

"Damn it, Rick," DB hollered.

"It's okay boss. I got this," Betty said. Turning around, she swiped the glass into the garbage can with her towel.

"Now, you acknowledge me, Betty?" As soon as the words came out, I instantly regretted them. Instead, I turned my temper tantrum onto DB. "Stop treating me like a child." Scooting from the barstool, I almost fell to the ground but managed to catch myself before my knees landed on the floor.

"Sit down," DB demanded, forcefully pushing me back onto the barstool. "Aaron!" He hollered. "Can you take Rick home?"

"Sure," a voice from the back of the club. "Be right there in a few."

"I'm going to go," Kingston said. Removing his baseball hat, he passed a hand over his head, then put it back on.

"That's probably for the best," DB said with no feeling.

"Rick, I'll see you later. Sorry about your girlfriend," he said as he left the club.

Anger consumed as I watched Kingston leave. I wanted to ask DB what his beef with Kingston was but I had other things on my mind.

Chorus
Baron Samedi

My door opened to reveal a man standing there in a pair of wingtips. He wore a suit with an ascot around his neck. Even I knew not to look at his face.

The man walked in and sat down. I offered him a cigar and cut the tip off without hesitation. He took it and sat in the chair and crossed his legs.

"Sir, what can I do for you today?"

"You can tell me why Kingston Dupe is visiting the Dead Creole Club asking for help?"

I shook my head, causing the skeletons on my top hat to shudder in fear. "I had no idea he was doing such things."

"You need to keep your humans in check."

"Yes, but Kingston isn't one of mine."

"Well, find someone to keep him in line. He owes me quite a bit of money.

"I will, sir."

"Good, don't make me come back down here." He stood and left without another word.

After he left, Skeley peeked out from his painting and asked, "Who the hell was that?" His voice shook. I was a shocked.

"Just an old friend. It's a story for another day," I said, relaxing back into my wingback chair and puffing on my cigar to calm my nerves.

"How in the hell did I ever get mixed up with him?" I wondered.

Fifteen minutes later

A knock echoed on my door.

"Come in," I said, sitting behind my desk.

Elvis popped his head around the door. "May I come in?"

"Sure." I waved, but he stood just outside the doorway. "Does Guede Nibo know you're here again?"

"Yes, I told him I was coming to visit you."

"Good, good. Come in my boy, my boy."

But he stopped dead in his tracks.

"What's wrong?" I asked.

"You sounded like someone I used to know."

I stood, met him at the doorway, grabbed him by the shoulder. and ushered him inside. Grinning, I asked, "Who? The Colonel? Pay no mind to my babbling. Here sit." He sat as I instructed him but with a little hesitation. I leaned against the desk. "So, what prompts another visit from the King of Rock and Roll?"

"Not sure." He leaned back in the chair, stretching out his

long legs. "I guess a feeling of unsettledness came over me, and I can't seem to shake it."

I didn't dare tell him his feeling of uneasiness was probably due to being separated from his other half and it was close to his birthday. After all, he was used to being inside a tribute. Maybe watching one of them again would help ease the anxiousness feeling. "Would you like to watch the veil again?"

"Yes I would." He smiled that dazzling smile though it had a hint of nervousness to it.

I waved my hand. The air shimmered, then revealed a scene in front of us. As we sat watching, I felt a little sorry for the humans and their emotions. What a pity to have to deal with death like that. Down here, we didn't deal with death. It just was. It was the end of things.

I watched Elvis ensconced in the young man drowning his heartbreak in a bottle. As I watched, I was thankful I wasn't human. Elvis remained in his seat, stunned, watching Rick's actions.

"I wonder how he's going to get over this?" Elvis turned to me, sadness written on his face. "You know, losing someone like that."

I shrugged my shoulders. "Perhaps as any human does. Let's liven up this macabre time with a little music and a little dancing." I smiled and waved my hand toward the gramophone. The song 'It's All Because of You' began to play.

Little one popped out of her hiding spot with a creepy grin upon her face. I laughed and nodded over to Elvis. "This should be nice. I wonder what they will perform for us?"

A male skeleton came out and took Little One by the hand. They slowly moved across the desk forward then sideways.

RICK THE DEAD CREOLE CLUB

I could watch the sky dim and fade
Who needs it anyway?
It's all because of you

THE TWO SKELETONS moved in sync then the male dipped her. She smiled at me. When he swung her again, they moved around my desk, dancing a two-step.

Cause every touch and every word
It's my entire world
It's all because of you

Forever is right now
Nothing left behind
All others forgotten
You own this heart and mind

THE TWO LITTLE skeletons moved in sync across the desk as if they were floating.

There is love here for the taking
Dreams in the making
It's all because of you

. . .

Forever is right now
Nothing left behind
All others forgotten
You own this heart and mind

THE TWO LITTLE skeletons were mesmerizing as they moved in front of us. I don't know about Elvis, but I couldn't take my eyes off them.

There is love here for the taking
Dreams in the making
It's all because of you
It's all because of you

ONCE THE SONG WAS OVER, they both bowed. Elvis and I clapped joyously. "Bravo, bravo!" I kept an eye on Elvis to make sure the dance had kept him occupied. However, I could tell he was still stealing peaks at the opened veil. I should have closed it, but what was done was done.

I returned my attention back to the little skeletons. Little One sauntered over and waved at me with a finger wave.

"What is it?" I bent down to her level.

"Ahh, so that is it. I will tell him," I whispered to her. Her tiny white face turned a crimson red as she covered it with her tiny hands. She immediately ran back to her hidey hole, but her face turning a bright, cherry red was not lost on me.

I tapped my bony fingers on the desk. "It appears that they are learning ballroom dances and would love it if you would be here for the next one. Apparently, they are big fans of yours, as well."

"Ahem." Skeley cleared his throat. We both turned our heads in his direction. "Big boss man, that might be my doing." He smiled and then returned to the book he was reading as he sat under a huge oak tree, its branches swaying in the breeze.

"Is that so, Skeley?"

He grinned with satisfaction.

I grimaced, knowing that the backlash would be detrimental to my well-being if Erik found out. "Skeley, you really should not have."

"Why not?" He said, not even pulling his attention from his book. "Are you afraid of Erik being jealous?"

"No." I lied.

"Well, he has no reason to be. All I did was tell them about your guest sitting in the chair," He said, peeking over the cover of the book.

"When did you have time to tell them? Oh, never mind…"

He scoffed. "When you took the missus on vacation. I was bored and we talked about lots of things." He returned to his book.

I sure as hell did not want to deal with Erik's jealousy. I am sure he already had it in his head that I favored Skeley over him.

I focused my attention back on Elvis. "Well, what do you say?"

He chuckled. "It would be my pleasure, as long as I'm here and if you allow it."

I watched as Little One peeked from her hiding spot and

eerily grinned from ear to ear at the news. I shook my head, but Elvis's excitement was not lost on me. I knew it was something he secretly thrived on. How could I take this away from him?

Bitter they Are, Harder They Fall

Rick

JANUARY 8TH

"DB, I will not be treated like a child." My words tended to slur more the angrier I became.

"Rick, you will not put your life or anyone else's in danger by doing something stupid. Aaron, will take you home," he demanded.

"Fine." I hissed and stood shakily, but stood nonetheless, and waited for my ride home.

Aaron came out from the back. "Are you ready to go?"

"Sure." I steadied myself, but not too well. I wobbled back and forth, grabbing onto the edge of the bar to balance myself.

"Here, let me help you. What all have you had to drink?" Aaron asked.

Betty turned around and chuckled. "Everything."

"Oh, now she speaks." My sarcasm was on point tonight. Betty glared at me.

"Rick, I cut you off because I care about you," she said, turning around and speaking to her imaginary friend again.

"Come on let's go, Aaron," I spat angrily.

Ten minutes later

The second I stepped outside, I threw up all over Aaron's shoes. I wasn't the least bit surprised when he cursed. "Son of a bitch, Rick. Couldn't you have moved over at least three inches?" He tried to shake off his shoe and looked at it in disgust.

"I'm sorry," I said, wiping my mouth with the back of my hand.

"It's fine. Just get in the damn car." He shoved me inside, but it took forever. I kept throwing up, and he had to make sure I didn't throw up in his precious truck. Once I felt everything was gone from my stomach, I sighed and looked at Aaron. When it was safe, I slumped against the seat and closed my eyes. I desperately wanted the pain to go away, but the numbness I tried to create started to dissipate.

Then, to make matters worse, I was starting to get a massive headache. And honestly, my breath didn't smell too great.

"Rick, if you have the urge to throw up again, by God, you better fucking tell me, or I'll kick you out and make you walk the fuck home."

"Aye aye sir." I gave him a half assed salute.

Aaron put the truck into gear and the hum of the engine started to lull me to sleep like a lullaby. When he pulled away from the curb, my eyes grew heavy. I could no longer keep them open. He turned onto the street and my eyes had shut. Before I knew it, I was out cold.

"Rick, wake up." Aaron nudged me. I tried to pry my eyes open, but the alcohol had an intense hold on me. "Come on Rick let's get you inside. He nudged me again and this time I had to force my eyes open and thank goodness it was dark outside, though the streetlights didn't help the headache that was growing to plant itself in my cranium. "I carefully scooched out of the truck so not to embarrass myself in front of my neighbors who had just stepped outside of their house.

"Hi Mrs. Coleman. I waved to her as she sneered at me.

"They need to keep the riff raff out of the neighborhood." She huffed as she hobbled down the uneven sidewalk.

"Ole biddy never liked me any way," I said under my breath.

Aaron shook his head as he helped me up the steps. "Where's your keys?"

"Oh shit," I mumbled as I dug in my pockets. "Damn it! I must have left them inside," I sighed, remembering I'd walked to the club when I felt the necessity to drink my woes away. "Just knock on the door. Jacob should be home. I know he left the club hours ago."

Leaning against the door, I instantly wanting to throw up, the impulses coming to me in waves as we waited for Jacob to open the door. Suddenly, I leaned over the cast iron railing and released the contents of my stomach into the bushes. I was surprised I had anything left since I had thrown up so much in front of the club.

"Hey, how is he doing?" Jacob asked as he opened the door.

Pulling back from the railing, I wiped my mouth with the back of my hand and grumbled, "I'm doing just fine." Then pushed my way past Jacob.

"Jacob, please keep an eye on him. DB and the rest of us will check on him tomorrow. DB also said he will be in contact with Josephine's parents about the funeral."

"I will," Jacob said as I stumbled to my room.

"I do not need a damn babysitter," I moaned loudly, slamming my bedroom door.

Flopping down on my bed, I wondered if it was true, or could it all be a farce? Josephine couldn't be… I couldn't bear to utter the words. She was supposed to be coming home soon. I was going to propose to her. We were going to be happy.

A low knock on the door resonated through my room. "Rick, there's some mail for you," Jacob said, slowly opening my door. "May I come in?" He asked.

At first, I didn't answer him, just continued staring at the ceiling fan, spinning in a clockwise direction that almost hypnotized me. The room started to swirl, and I was desperately trying to stop it. I closed my eyes before I hurled again. Placing a hand on my stomach, I hoped it would stop the rumbling and the bile from rising and making another appearance.

"Yes," I mumbled almost incoherently.

Inching into my room, he stood there with an envelope in his right hand. "Here, this came for you today."

When I didn't answer or move, he placed it on the bed beside me.

"Thank you," I whispered, barely recognizing my own voice. I glanced over and saw the Germany address, but I couldn't make myself pick it up. I laid there, sprawled on my bed, remembering the second time I'd seen her…

It was before I met DB. I had just started performing as Elvis. Geeze. It felt like an eternity.

I STEPPED onto the stage at Storck Barracks. The audience was filled with army men and women, but one and only one stood out to me.

The one from Bad Naheuim. I couldn't believe she was there. How could I be so lucky?

I was so shocked that I forgot the words to the song I was supposed to be singing, but instead of panicking, I just stood there. The more I tried to remember the words, the more they refused to return. It didn't matter how much I begged, they simply wouldn't come back.

"Rick, what's wrong?" Zerrin asked, trying to get my attention from the wings.

Spinning to face him, I nodded in the direction of the audience. Grabbing the green army curtains, he peeked out and saw what had my attention, then grinned and mouthed, "You've got this."

I stared out at the crowd and before they could start throwing tomatoes or other vegetables at me, I quickly regained my composure. Shaking my left leg to the familiar tune I'd sung more times than I could count, I let the music move through my entire body. Glancing out into the audience when my song was almost over, I pulled the scarf from my neck. The girls rushed to the stage, but I had eyes for only one girl. Walking to the edge of the stage, I nodded to her, smiled, and wrapped it around her neck.

After the show was over, I had to meet her. "Zerrin, I need to find her."

"Who?" He asked.

I laughed. "You know who–the girl."

"You mean her?" He pointed.

"She's behind me, isn't she?"

He nodded, grinning wide. "Looks like she found you," he winked, then walked off, leaving me to talk to my dream girl.

I turned around and there she was. "Hi." She smiled. "Your show was amazing. I wanted to tell you how much I enjoyed it." Her cheeks started turning a bright red.

"Thank you. What's your name?" I asked her.

"Josephine."

I nodded. "So, wanna go out sometime?" I wasn't going to let her slip through my fingers.

The smile that crept across her face elated me. "Sure, I'd love to.

As the memory faded, I sat up in bed, knowing I had to get out of the house. It was horribly stifling. I stood, and although I was still a little wobbly, I managed to make it out of my room without bumping into any walls. Then I remembered the letter, so I stumbled back to my room, grabbing my jacket and the letter. Quickly stuffing it into my pocket, I left.

Jacob was nowhere to be seen. I assumed he was fast asleep in his room. Grabbing my keys, I headed outside, careful not to make noise. Locking the door back, I made my way to my 1968 Mustang Fastback. Sliding a hand over her green paint job, I stuck the key into the lock. Before I could open the door, I felt a knife pushed into my side.

"Give me all of your money and your keys," the shaky voice said as the guy jabbed me.

"Oh shit."

A warm liquid dripped down my side. I was too drunk to deal with this. Slowly turning, I tried not to make matters worse. "Look, you can have whatever you want," I reassured, handing him my keys.

The roaring sound of motorcycles shattered our tenuous stalemate. It was so loud I was so sure my neighbors would be coming out to see what was happening.

But they didn't, and the would-be mugger still held the knife on me. Even though his head was somewhat covered, I got a good glimpse of him. Face covered with acne, he couldn't be but seventeen.

Or was I still drunk? No. I was suddenly sobering up.

The guy was scared, and I was his scapegoat since the motorcycle guys stopped and came for him. The look in his eyes was that of a wild animal. His head bounced one way and the other as he glanced between me and them.

Then he did the unthinkable.

I knew it was only out of fright, but the guy took the knife and sliced across my throat. Before I hit the ground, I got a glimpse of my saviors.

In an instant, a thought popped in my head–I was going to die. Then I thought, "Oh shit, if I die, I'm never going to be able to sing again."

Then everything went dark, and I was thrown to the ground. The side of my face hit the street. My attacker screamed in agony as he was ripped away from me. I lay on the ground beside my car on the cold pavement wishing I'd stayed in my house as everything went black and I passed out.

Chorus
Baron Samedi

January 8th

I leaned back in my chair contemplating what had been happening here in the Underworld lately. But as Skeley read his book and I remembered Erik was not here, something drew my attention to the veil that was still open.

Elvis, who still sat in front of me, focused on it as well. "What is he thinking? I mean he shouldn't be getting into that car. He's been drinking."

Elvis's attention was drawn forward as he sat on the edge of his chair, bracing his hands on his knees. Chuckling, I followed Elvis' gazed to see what he was watching.

Rick was stumbling out to his car. "You know by the looks of it, I think he is."

Turning, Elvis stared at me for a second, then returned to the veil. "Can't you do anything?

"Of course, I could." I leaned back in my chair, a feeling of glee overtaking me.

"What can you do for him?"

I cocked my head. "It depends on what you want me to do." My comment was void of any emotion.

"Can't you stop him from getting into the car? He's drunk."

I arched my brow at him. "Be careful what you ask of me."

"What do you mean?"

"I guess I could help, but it would be my choice in what way."

"What do you mean?" He turned away from me to stare into the hazy screen. For a split second he glanced over his shoulder, taking his attention off the tribute who was trying to get into his car.

"Elvis, remember when I said I could change things with the snap of my fingers?"

"Yes, I do."

"Well, I can, but you may not like what I do."

"He could have Rick hurt or worse," Skeley spoke from his post in his painting.

Elvis turned to face the painting then looked back at me, gasping. "You wouldn't?"

My smile turned maniacal, but before I could respond, Skeley answered, "Oh, he would."

Shock registered on Elvis' face. "You would do that?"

"Ignore Skeley, but yes, I would."

Leaning forward, I smiled. Raising my hand, I snapped my fingers. Elvis spun his head back in the direction of the veil. He gasped when a masked man walked up to Rick and held a knife to his side. He sucked in an audible breath as the knife-wielding mad man sliced Rick across his throat and let him drop to the ground.

Elvis dropped his head into his lap, fearful to look at the accident I had caused with a snap of my fingers. With his face hidden he asked. "Is he dead?"

"We can only hope that he's on the brink of it." I grinned wickedly.

"What good will he be if he's dead?"

"Oh, come on. You haven't forgotten how this works, have you? Don't be getting soft on me now."

"No, I just didn't realize you actually killed them."

"Well, I didn't kill the other two, I had help." I laughed. "And I am going to help Rick come to me, so to speak," I chuckled, standing from my comfortable chair.

"Why would you do that?" He asked, lifting his eyes to face me.

I laughed haughtily. "Because Mr. Presley, I cannot always depend on Mr. King to bring me a tribute and have you forgotten what today is?" I sneered at him for a second.

He looked forlorn. "Oh, shit I had. Time seems to get away from me here. It's my birthday, isn't it?"

I nodded. "And I am sure Mr. King did as well with everything going on with Mr. Miceli out there." I waved at the veil as what happened next was something I hadn't planned. Instantly enraged, I continued to speak while watching the motorcycle club drag the poor, unsuspecting knife-wielding mad man away. "So, I would just let him fall into my lap." I sat back in my red wing chair and continued to puff on my cigar. "That was not expected."

"Who is that?" Skeley interrupted, looking over the binding of his book.

"That, my dear friend, is Elek, president of the Beast of Atonement Motorcycle Club."

"So, what are you going to do?" He asked me as a muscular man scooped up the mugger as if he weighed nothing and tossed him against a tree.

"What are you going to do about that?" Elvis asked.

"I'm going to go and tell him to mind his own damn business." I stood.

"What about Rick?" Skeley asked not bothering to put his book down.

About that time, Erik finally deemed it necessary to enter my office with a damn cell phone pressed to his nonexistent ear. "Well, yes, as soon as you hear anything let me know." Hanging up the phone, he looked at us.

"Who was that?" I asked, still standing but getting exponentially tired of the ongoing chaos in my world that I vowed to handle when I got back.

"Lawson. He's still searching for Selvis but he hasn't seen or heard from him. If fact, no one's seen him. We've checked with all the gate keepers." His attention was suddenly distracted by the King of Rock and Roll. "Uh, why is he sitting in my chair?" His tone said he was put off that someone was taking up his precious space. Crossing his bony arms over his chest, he stuck out his bottom lip.

"Find another place to sit, Erik," I grumbled. "I do not have time for this. I must go get a tribute." I grabbed my staff, but before leaving, I leaned in real close to my first in command. "You make sure nothing happens to Mr. Presley. You guard him with your life." Stepping back, I stabbed the ground with my staff.

Erik glared at Elvis for a split second. Then he caught my look as I stomped my staff for the seventh time, and quickly changed it as I disappeared.

"What how am... guard... him?" I heard his voice echo into

the distance, but it was too late to answer him. So, he'd better figure it out.

All Shook Up

Rick

I LAY ON THE GROUND, blood pooling all around me. Suddenly, a panic rose as I dug into my pocket for the letter from Josephine. It was nowhere to be found. "What the hell?" I muttered to myself.

"Hey, are you all right?" I heard someone ask me.

"Damn it, Elek. Why the hell are you interfering in my business?"

I tried to roll over to see who was speaking but it was hard. I had a huge gash in my neck. Placing my hand over the wound, I pressed as hard as I could to stop the bleeding.

When I thought I accomplished something, I tried to roll over. I saw a huge muscular man standing beside a motorcycle with his arms crossed over his broad chest.

But what was more interesting was the man–or thing–he was talking to. It was the skeletal man. I sighed deeply, making my neck wound throb all the more.

"Seriously, Baron Samedi, what the hell are you doing with this guy?" The motorcycle guy pointed in my direction.

"That, Elek, is none of your business. Now, return to your club and let me get back to my dealing with my man here."

"Fine, but if I find out you are up to no good, my mother will hear about this."

"Tell your mother I said hello," the bone man said.

Coldness wrapped around my body and my eyelids grew heavy. I could barely hold them open.

The man called Elek straddled his motorcycle. It roared to life as he threatened, "Baron Samedi, you better take care of that boy."

"Elek, watch who you are threatening." The bone man's voice was crystal clear as I struggled on the ground and my body grew colder.

"Wake up, Mr. Miceli," a deep voice commanded.

I tried to open my eyes, but they wouldn't budge.

It felt like something was sitting on my chest. When I tried to move, I started to panic. "Why can't I open my eyes?" I yelled aloud.

"Try harder. Mr. Miceli," the voice instructed.

I tried to move my arms, but they were pinned to my sides. However, this time, my eyes opened a pinch, and I gasped hoarsely.

Turning my head to see where the voice came from, tremors shook my body as fear rolled through me. All I could do was stare at a skeletal man, kneeling on the concrete between me and my car.

This was the bone man who killed Robin. He was going to bring trouble to the club. Everything that happened was his fault.

"Are you here to kill me?" I choked out the words, barely able to speak.

"No, you've done that on your own." He stood, danced a

little as he stared up at the night sky. Such a nice night for death, isn't it?" he said casually as grinned down at me. He tipped his hat at me. "Maybe you never should have left your house. However, if you have learned anything from Jesse it is that you can't change your fate, can you?" Leaning against my mustang, he tipped his hat as his white gloved hand rubbed the brim, bringing the little skeletons sitting around it to life.

With every touch, they chomped at his hand and made munching noises. He chuckled eerily. "Well, to be honest, I may have helped a little."

It had to be a dream. I wanted to wake up. I nervously grinned at him. "Why would you do that?"

"Because I needed your help with something," he laughed.

"What if I don't want to help you?" I tried to turn away, to move at all, but it was no use. I was stuck.

He laughed. "Oh, you will want to help me."

"What makes you say that?"

"Because I'm the only one who can bring you back from the dead." The skeletal man laughed at me.

"Wait! I'm dead?" I started to panic.

"You won't remain that way if you help me."

"Will I ever be able to sing again?"

He shrugged his shoulders. "That question, I have no answer for."

"So, wait, you did this to me and yet you can't tell me if my throat is damaged enough to cause permanent problems with me singing ever again?" I wanted to rip him apart.

He chuckled, the sound unlike anything I'd ever heard. It was like something out of a horror movie. Trying to sit up, I realized I couldn't. "What's wrong with me?" I tried to hide the panic in my voice.

"Nothing. I just want you still for what I'm going to ask."

I stared up at the dark sky. The stars winked back at me while I waited for the skeleton man to speak. "What do you want from me? Will it be a similar trick that you played on my friend, Robin?"

His laugh was eerie. It sent chills up and down my spine. Bending down, he was close enough for me to smell his putrid breath. Snickering, he taunted, "Your friend Robin's death was his destiny."

"You mean to tell me that Robin chose to die and live out his life stuck in the club?" I was angry, then a thought popped into my head. "Where is my letter?"

"I have it safe and sound. You humans and your love life." He patted his jacket. "No worries. It amazes me that your lives always revolve around a girl. And as for Robin, he didn't choose anything, it was his destiny. Now, back to more important things."

"Which are what?" I snapped, a little too sarcastically for the skeletal man's liking. I refused to look away, wanting our interaction to end so I could get back to Josphine.

"Well, as you know, Mr. King and I have a deal, but tonight is Mr. Presley's birthday and I can't depend on him all the time." He waved his hands. "But that's really not the point."

"What is?" I cynically asked.

Managing to face him, I saw his expression and immediately wished I had used a different tone. Closing my eyes, I and wished I'd made a different choice, but I knew it wouldn't change the outcome.

When I opened my eyes, he was staring at me, his eyes vacant. I waited for him to continue. I knew he wanted to reprimand me but chose not to.

"Anyway, I need your help in something."

"Seriously?" I almost chuckled but thought better of it.

The pain from my neck wound started to gain some traction, causing me to choke as I moved to stare back at the sky again. I did my best to ignore it as he once again began to speak.

"I need a tribute to help me find Elvis's other half–Selvis. Let me get you out of here and to the underworld with Elvis. It will be more comfortable to sign the contracts in my office."

I blinked my eyes, not believing what was happening. I still didn't believe that Jesse and Robin had Elvis's soul inside them. "But what if I don't...?"

Before I could finish my sentence, I was suddenly whisked from the street. The pain was subliminal. The sensation my body going through whatever I went through was surreal.

Chorus

Baron Samedi

IN THE BLINK OF AN EYE, I stood in the hallway leading to my office. Leaning on my staff, the seven skeletons rattled in defiance.

"What is wrong with you all? Is something going on?" They didn't answer, just kept up their incessant rattling.

Holding onto Rick like a ragdoll, I quickly plopped him in a chair outside my office. The door was ajar, and I peeked inside.

It was empty. No Erik. No Elvis. What the hell? I gasped in horror.

"Erik, where the hell are you?" Yelling, panic set in.

Stepping back outside, I looked for any sign of my first in command or Elvis. I saw nothing. Waiting for a moment, I impatiently tapped my foot. I watched Rick, slumped in the chair, void of any emotion.

"Don't worry, it won't be much longer. Then we will get down to business."

After what felt like an eternity, especially in the Underworld, Erik came running around the corner. "You called for me?" He panted, pausing to place a hand to his chest.

"Where the hell have you been?"

"I... uh..." he stammered.

"Never mind. Can you help him into the office?" I waved my hand at Rick who looked like he was going to throw up at any moment.

"Rick. please do not throw up in my office. If you have the urge, use the trash bin." He bobbed his head up and down like one of those dolls.

Erik struggled, helping Rick up from the chair "Does he have to be so heavy?" He griped loudly.

I glared at him, and he instantly shut up.

Rick rocked back and forth, almost causing Erik to topple backward. I caught them both before they fell.

"What happened to him?" Erik asked exasperated.

"Ah, he had a little accident."

Erik stopped trying to hold Rick still and stared at me. "Are you serious?" His tone was also indignant, but he caught himself. "Did you cause said accident?"

"And what if I did?" I leaned on my staff, daring Erik to give me lip.

Painstakingly, he held the tribute up, knowing he didn't dare answer.

"Come on, let's get him into the office. We have plenty to

discuss." I followed Erik as he dragged Rick into the office. Before Erik had Rick seated in a chair, I turned, walked toward the painting and asked the burning question, my eyes turning red. "Where the hell did Elvis go?".

"I have no idea," Skeley replied, not looking up from his latest book.

"What the hell do you mean?"

"I mean, I have no idea where your precious King of Rock and Roll went. You didn't leave me in charge of his well-being," he sarcastically replied. "You left that duty to Erik." Waving his hand toward my first in command, Skeley still didn't look up from his book.

"Are you jealous I didn't leave you in charge?" I asked, ignoring his offended tone.

Turning his back on me, still reading his book, he answered, "All I can say is I would've made sure Elvis was here when you got back with your tribute."

I shook with rage. It was a strange, unusual feeling, I had had enough.

"Erik!" My voice echoed off the walls. Skeley painting went askew on the wall. I glared at Erik as he helped Rick into a chair, placing my hands on my hips.

"Yes, sir." His head whipped up to stare at me, almost dropping Rick on the floor. Struggling to regain a hold on the tribute, he stuttered.

"Where is Elvis?" I meandered over to him, speaking in a sing song voice. I decided to handle Erik with kid gloves. He was obviously nervous. After all, he almost dropped Rick on the floor.

His eyes went wide. "He's... uh... he's... uh... he's not here?" He stuttered.

"Do you see him anywhere here?" I smiled as I bent at the

waist, twisting my head from side to side and waving both arms.

Trying to humor me, he looked around. "No, Baron Samedi, I don't see him." His legs shook uncontrollably.

"Then where is he?" I shrieked, causing the walls to tremble.

He shrugged his shoulders, but I didn't know if it was out of fear or because he had no idea where Elvis was.

"Erik, you had one job. To keep an eye on Mr. Presley."

Hs shaking intensified. His legs knocked together. He let go of Rick who collapsed to the floor. Ignoring the poor soul crumpled under the chair, I focused on Erik as he stuffed his bony hands into his pockets, a nervous habit. "Yes... uh... but Lawson called with information on Selvis. So... uh... I told Elvis not to leave." He abashedly peered around.

"Damn it, Erik! My wife had better not have gotten him."

His eyes went wide with fear and his knees knocked even louder.

"Geeze, and he whines when I scream, but I have to listen to that knockin?" Skeley piped up.

"Damn it. Skeley! Shut up the fuck up," I grumbled loudly.

"Baron Samedi, she was not here. I swear." Erik started to cry.

"Erik, you'd better tell him the truth." Skeley spoke from his painting.

My head spinning around, I demanded, "What the hell is going on here?"

"Your... uh... well... uh she uh came ... in here," Erik stuttered.

"Spit it out," I raged.

"Erik, ran out and left your previous commodity sitting here when your wife came looking for you," Skeley tattled.

Turning towards the painting, the walls shook with my fury. "Why the hell didn't you tell me, Skeley?" I was instantly furious with him.

"Like I said, not my circus, not my crazy. So, I repeat not my problem."

"Um... maybe he just stepped out for a breather or maybe he went back to Guede Nibo," Erik said, still shaking, his bony legs knocking together like maracas.

"If you'd have left me in charge this wouldn't have happened," Skeley interjected, not looking up from his book.

Erik glared at the painting. "Shut up," he growled at him through tears.

"Enough you two, we have company."

Glancing to the side, I saw Rick still laying on a heap on the floor. From his position, his eyes went wide as he stared at the two skeletons hashing it out in front of him.

"Where am I?" His whisper was barely audible.

"What did you say?" Not waiting for an answer, I continued, "We'll deal with this when I get back." Scooping him off the floor, I unceremoniously plopped him back into the chair.

"I have to find Elvis. I'll be right back. You two keep an eye on our company, or else," I threatened, stomping out in a huff.

FIFTEEN MINUTES later

COMING upon Guede Nibo's gate, I entered, careful not to touch the little skeletons along the cast iron gate. One of them scampered to the top and lashed out. I popped him on the head with my staff.

"No, you will not," I chastised.

Bowing at me, the little bugger hugged himself in sorrow. As I entered, I groaned in relief when I heard Elvis singing a beautiful song. Continuing, I was shocked to see all the chairs removed and the usual audience dancing a waltz to the song *This is Our Dance.*

Elvis stood on the stage belting out the serene lyrics as the skeleton couples moved in sync to his words. It was beautiful and macabre at the same time. I was in awe and almost didn't notice my wife before she tapped me on the shoulder. "May I have this dance?" She asked.

"Of course, my dear," I said, taking her in my arms and moving her across the floor with the others. "To what do I owe the pleasure of seeing you here?"

Nodding in the direction of the stage, she explained, "I saw him in your office. He said he was waiting for you but could wait no longer. He asked if I would like to see him perform."

"Did he?" I nervously grinned.

"I thought," she paused and licked her lips. "Why not? I should see what the fuss is all about him."

Feeling her body, her bosom pressed against my body, I spun her around the room. "And what do you think?" I prodded.

"I want in on what you are doing with these guys and Elvis."

"No!" I spun her around on the floor.

"Why not?" She whined in protest.

"Because I said so."

Pulling away from me, she held me at arm's length. "Why not?" She pushed out her bottom lip.

Pulling her back to me, I sweetly asked, "My dearest, can't you find your own hobby to be fascinated with?"

"I guess so," she cooed, pushing away from me once again.

Watching her walk off, I smiled as she stopped just short of the shadows, turned to me, waved, and then left. That woman is up to something, but I had no idea what.

Shaking my head, I went up to the stage. "Elvis, come, I need to see you."

Smiling weakly, he jumped from the stage. "You know I'd rather perform at the International. Too much drama happens here," he said, following me.

I cocked a brow in his direction, I chose to ignore his comment.

Fifteen minutes later

Returning to my office, I stayed silent as I walked. Many thoughts plagued my mind. I needed to find a way to stop my wife from spying on me. A spell would be best. I didn't have time to visit Rosie, but I figured I had enough power to whip up a little rhyme of my own to do the job.

All I could do was think about the spell I needed to say to protect us from my wife. I knew she wouldn't stop trying to get into what we were doing. Stopping right in front of the wooden office door, I made sure Elvis and I were alone.

"We aren't going in?" He asked.

I spun on my heels and faced him. "Not yet. I need to know—what did my wife ask you?"

Utter shock crossed his face. "She asked me what we were doing."

"What did you tell her?" I hoped for the best-case scenario.

"Nothing. I knew not to tell her anything." He bit his bottom lip, drawing it down into a straight, thin line.

I couldn't tell if he was lying. I hoped he wasn't. I had to trust him if our friendship was going to last. Did we have a friendship? I thought I wanted one, so, I took what he said had face value.

"I believe you."

"Good." He put his hand on the doorknob, but I stopped him with a shake of my head. Pulling his hand back, he stuffed it in his pockets and waited.

Raising my arms high above my head, the sleeves of my jacket slid down my bony arms and I proceeded to chant a spell to protect all that were inside.

Later, I would do one for the club.

Darkness protects those who make a deal
   A song places the king of rock in those who wish to heal
   One who wishes ill to these two bound.
   Must never know how they are to be crowned.

Once the spell was said, I felt satisfied that as long as we were in my office Elvis and whatever tribute were safe from anyone finding out what I was doing. With the protection spell set, we went into my office.

Edge of Reality
Rick

As I lay on the floor, unable to move, dark shadows followed me. I wondered what kept them at bay. Gaping at the macabre office with its black painted walls trimmed in a deep purple and array of skulls hung ceremoniously in weird fashions, I tried to speak, but my mouth was too dry. I could only watch the two skeletons arguing.

I sat on the edge of reality. The bone man and his skeletons were all around, tormenting me with their morbid conversation.

"Dammit," I thought to myself. "I must have lost quite a lot of blood when my neck was slashed." Reaching up, I touched the gash in my neck, but my hand came back clean. "This can't be possible," I spoke aloud, my voice sounding hoarse.

The skeletal man turned to me. "Did you say something?" His tone was eerie. Quickly pulling me from the floor, he stuffed me back into the chair.

Shaking my head, I was fearful to say anything. Thankfully, he left in a huff.

Sitting there, I wondered how I could leave. Then my eyes met the young skeleton. He was glaring at me with his arms crossed. I figured the best thing to do was to just remain seated.

After fifteen minutes or so, the door opened. In walked none other than the King of Rock and Roll himself followed by the bone man. I almost fell out of the chair all over again–but it could have been from the amount of blood I'd lost.

"Yes, that's really him." A voice behind me answered the question I hadn't asked.

Trying to look behind me, I quickly gave up. I couldn't move my neck like that was not a possibility it hurt like a bitch.

"You're wondering if that's really Elvis, aren't you?" The voice asked.

This time I pushed through the pain and turned around in the chair. There was no one but a little skeleton waving from a painting.

"Skeley, stop that." The bone man angrily demanded.

"Why? I know he was wondering if Elvis was real. You were, weren't you?" He asked, smiling eerily.

Slumping back into the chair, I wondered what fresh hell I was in. Maybe I was dreaming–or it was more of a nightmare. Closing my eyes, I mentally wondered, if I wake up, will all of this will go away? Maybe if I said it over and over, I'd wake back up in my bed. Much like Dorothy in the Wizard of Oz. Maybe it would be as if I never left my house, tried to get into my car, a mugger slashed my neck. and I bled out.

"No, it won't. That won't help." the little skeleton cackled.

My eyes popped open. I was still in the same chair and the bone man was still staring at me. He walked forward toward me, but Elvis remained by the door leaning against it in all his glory.

I Can Help You
Baron Samedi

"Rick, as I told you..." I glowered at the others, "We need your help, to find Selvis."

"How do you propose I do that?" I wondered out loud.

"With his help." He waved a hand toward the man leaning against the door frame.

"And just how do you plan on him helping me?"

I laughed. "You know how the others had it done. They had Elvis placed inside of them. Don't play dumb with me Mr. Maceli."

He stared at me but it was not a look of shock but one of defiance. "No, I don't want this. I don't want Elvis inside me. I don't want to perform anymore."

"Why not?" Elvis asked, turning leaning on the door, propping one leg against it.

Sitting forward, Rick heaved a heavy sigh. "Because I've lost everything and frankly, I don't feel it anymore. It's not worth it."

"But why not? I thought as a tribute it was something you enjoyed. Paying tribute to my life, my legacy."

He sat there carefully contemplating his next words, so as not to offend anyone. "Because I don't think I'd enjoy it anymore." he finally answered.

"Maybe I could entice you with something." I pulled the letter from my coat pocket. "What if I let you read this after you accomplished what I ask of you?" I waved the envelope in his face.

He grabbed at it, but I pulled it away quickly.

"Tsk tsk. Not until you finish what I ask of you." I smiled.

Slumping, he murmured, "Fine. Whatever. Iit's probably the only way I'm getting out of here anyway, right?"

"Well, it sort of is. I mean you are in the Underworld, after all. There are only two ways out."

"Which are?" He sarcastically asked.

Glaring at him for a second, I decided to give him my knowledge because of all he'd gone through. "One is through the seventh gate." I cocked my head. "But that's not the wisest choice."

"And the second one?" He coaxed.

Tapping a bony finger on the desk, I pointed to Elvis and grinned.

"Can I make a counteroffer?" He asked.

I chuckled. "Well, that my dear boy, is nervy, but go ahead." I rubbed my chin. "Let's hear what you have to say."

"Can't you bring my girlfriend back from the dead?"

My eyes went wide, and Skeley gasped. I glared at him to shut up and he did. Leaning toward Rick, he slid further back in the chair.

"My boy, my boy, I am afraid that ship has sailed." Standing up straight, I pondered the new predicament. "But what if I counter your offer?"

"What are you offering?"

He was intrigued. I had him on the hook.

"What if I gave you the option to say goodbye after her funeral." I glanced at clock on the wall. Instead of telling time, it told days.

"Don't do it," Skeley muttered. "It's a trick."

"Shut up, Skeley." I scowled at the little skeleton on the wall.

Rick did not bother to turn and look at the painting. "Wait. Can I do that?"

The smile etched across my face was eerie, but Rick did not notice it. He was too wrapped up in the possibility of seeing his dead loved one. "Of course, you can. I will come for you when she's ready."

"So, what's the catch?" He stopped, waiting for me to answer. Then he added. "I know there's a catch. There's always a catch. There was one with my friends, Robin, Aaron, and DB. So, what is the catch?" He was relentless.

Smiling, I turned to Erik. "This one's smart, isn't he?" I grinned at him..

Erik nodded, but pouted and crossed his arms. I was sure it was because Rick still sat in his chair.

"Certainly, there will be a catch. When making a deal with me, you must be willing to accept the catch. Now, let's talk business." I whipped the ever-popular scroll out of thin air and handed it to Rick. Please read this over carefully. I would hate to be accused of trickery." My smile curved up at the corners of my mouth.

Taking the paper, he held it gently in his hands and read.

. . .

I, Rick Maceli, agree to let Elvis inhabit me. In return, I will help Baron Samedi, loa of the dead, find Selvis. In the event that I fail, Baron Samedi has the right to pick my punishment.

Addendum: After the funeral the party of this contract will be allowed to go to the seventh gate to say goodbye to his beloved.

SCRUTINIZING ME, he questioned, "Is this for real?"

"Why not? I am not heartless. I agree to your counteroffer but remember there's a catch." I grinned.

"Yes, but he is a..." Skeley started to speak. I glared at him and stopped him midsentence. "We don't need anything from the peanut gallery."

CONTINUING to look over the contract, he squinted his eyes and asked, "Hey what's this fine print?"

"Don't mind that. It will come to light when the time is right. Are you ready to sign?" I pulled out one of the skeletons from my staff. "Give me your finger." He did as I asked, and I stuck his finger. "Now, sign."

Watching as the blood bubbled to the surface of his forefinger, he quickly signed the paper and watched as his signature dried to a beautiful, golden color.

"Thank you," I said. Rolling it up, I went over to Skeley.

"Oh, great," Erik whined.

"What's the problem?" Rick asked, watching Erik clutch his nonexistent ears.

"Just wait," he muttered.

Skeley grinned, assumed his position, and turned into a combination dial.

"Do you really have to do this?" I shook my head, knowing the answer.

He nodded. "You know it. This is how I was made."

His grin widened from the shear excitement at what was about to happen. At every turn of the dial, Skeley screamed loudly. He enjoyed it way too much. Turning his dial one last time, his door swung open. Shoving Rick's contract inside, I turned around to see Erik, Rick and Elvis covering their ears.

"Just a little longer," I told them. Shutting the door, I gave Skeley three more spins and let him screech. "Okay, he's done."

I smiled as I watched Skeley return to his post under the tree. After a few seconds, he got up, walked to a boat, got in and paddled away.

Shrugging my shoulders, I walked back to Rick and Erik. "Rick, are you ready?"

"I guess I'm as ready as I can be." he mumbled.

"Good. Let me call, Sirene."

"Who's Sirene?" He asked.

"You will see." Skeley said, sitting under an oak tree with a book titled *The Protector's Kiss*.

In a flash, the beautiful Sirene appeared.

"Is that her?" Rick asked in awe.

Turning to him, I breathlessly responded, "Yes. Isn't she the most wonderous creature you have ever seen?" Looking over at Rick as he gaped, I clapped. "All right, let us get this started." I grinned.

"You called?" Her voice was melodic as the waves on the sea.

"Yes, Sirene."

"Baron Samedi, are we doing the same thing as before?"

"Yes, we are."

Winking at Elvis as he stood by the door, she smiled. Suddenly turning her attention to Rick, she cooed, "You must be the tribute who will house this gorgeous soul."

"Yes, ma'am," he said, his head popping up. "Will this hurt?" He asked me.

I shook my head. "No, it should not but I never had him put into me. So, I cannot really answer that question."

"Let's get this started." Sirene slowly exhaled. "I must get back to the water. I already feel like I'm starting to dry out." Leaning down, she ran her hand up and down her iridescent legs.

Perching herself upon my desk, she was careful not to sit on the spots containing my tiny skeletons. Her legs shone brightly, even in the dim lights of my office. I simply could not take my eyes off her beauty. "We should hurry then." I sat beside her and placed a bony hand on one of her legs. She trembled under my touch.

"Baron, I don't think your wife would appreciate you touching me." she winked at me.

I leaned in closer. "Let's not tell her then." I ran my hand up and down her silvery scaley legs. "It could be our little secret." I smiled.

Rick continued to stare, his eyes glazing over. I stood and faced him, I teased, "She is rather beautiful, is she not?"

He didn't say a single word, just nodded in agreement.

"Are you both ready?" Sirene asked.

Elvis stepped forward and stood beside Rick. "I'm ready. I'm... uh... sure that Rick is as well." He smiled that smile that made the girls go wild.

"Good." Sirene opened her mouth, the words enchanting as they flowed.

DIANA MARIE DUBOIS

. . .

♪ Morpheus comes
And peddles his dreams
Quilts of mist
With golden seams

Morpheus walks
On a path of bones
Of those who gambled
And sold their souls

To walk upon the earth again
To feel the wind on stolen skin
For just one glimpse of light
Free from their eternal night

Morpheus comes
To peddle his rhyme
To those who'll sign
On the dotted line

Morpheus knew
Every dream has a price

> He kisses your ear
> As he hands you the dice 🎵

Sirene's lips held the last of the words of the song. We were all captivated. Then she broke the spell by saying, "That should do it."

Rick searched my office with his eyes. "Where did he go?" He pointed to the door frame where Elvis used to be but was no more. Then looked beside him where just a few seconds before he had stood.

"Show him a mirror," Skeley quipped.

I don't have one," I mumbled.

"Sure, you do." Skeley grinned wide.

"Where?"

"Here in my painting."

"Ahaha!" I exclaimed. "I forgot." Taking Rick by the arm, I led him to the painting.

Skeley held up a mirror as Rick stared at the painting, muttering, "What the hell? This is the creepiest thing I've ever seen in my life."

I take offense to that, Elvis said.

"I didn't say you were creepy. Just that this whole thing *feels creepy*. To be honest, you look a little different than before." Swiveling his head to look at me, he asked, "Is this how you see him?"

"What do you mean you don't see him as a man of flesh, blood and bone?" I cocked my head at him wondering what Skeley was pulling.

"No, not in this mirror. I see him like I see you."

I glanced at Skeley and cocked my head. "Damn it! Stop

messing with him," I chastised without giving Rick a definite answer.

"Anyway." I slapped him on the back. "You will get used to it. The others did."

"Ahem. Can I get back to the quietness of the water?" Sirene interrupted us.

Spinning my alabaster head to face her, I acquiesced, "Oh, dear, where are my manners? Yes, you may."

And with that she disappeared in a flash.

"Elvis, I don't have to tie you to him, do I?"

No, I'll behave and stay inside him.

"Good."

Turning back to Rick, I said, "Now, to get you back home." I touched him and within seconds he was gone.

It Hurts Me

Rick

WHEN THE BONE man touched me, it felt like I was shoved into a tunnel. When I finally finished spinning, I'd landed on the street in front of the club. "Shit, why'd he put me here?"

Probably so DB could confront you about your indiscretions, The voice in my head spoke to me.

"Well, that is probably the truth," I grumbled.

I should warn you about one thing, don't talk to me out loud. The others will think you're crazy. Sooner or later, you will learn to talk to me in your head.

"Very true. I used to think Robin was out of his mind when I heard him talking to you." I sighed. "Well, let me get inside and get this over with." Opening the door, I almost jumped out of my skin.

What's wrong? Elvis asked me.

"I think I'm seeing things," I said, standing in the doorframe of the club. I couldn't move my feet. They were stuck in one place as if trapped in cement.

What's wrong? He asked me again.

I shook my head. "I can't believe Robin is sitting at the bar. He's dead, but I can see him."

That's because, at least, I'm betting, it's because you... uh... had a near death experience, and my soul is inside you. He explained.

"Well actually I died."

That explains why you are seeing him. Welcome to my world. Now, why don't you go say hi to him? He tried to push me forward. My feet moved a smidge. I assumed controlling the tributes got easier with each one. *I'm sure he'd appreciate it.*

My hand instinctually went to my throat. I felt the scar. It had to be a parting gift from the good old bone man himself.

Staring at my dead friend a little bit longer, I finally stepped further inside, allowing Elvis to lead me. I didn't see DB. Maybe I could talk to Robin for a bit before I was reprimanded. I walked up to the bar as soon as I did, Robin turned around and smiled as I approached.

At the sight of me, his eyes lit up. "Well, hello stranger. Does DB know you have a hitchhiker?"

"No, not yet." I sat down on a barstool and inspected the place.

"Don't worry. He's not here yet, but I'm assuming he will be upset when he finds out." Robin smiled over at Betty who had just come up to us.

"Why would he? Isn't that the deal he's made with the bone man...?" My train of thought was interrupted by Betty. "What the hell?" I gasped. Looking at her, I held onto the bar and tried not to fall off the barstool from shock.

"Hey, Rick, your usu...?" She paused. "Wait. You can see us in our natural form?"

"Apparently I can."

By the way, I should warn you, the band and backup singers are also skeletons. Oh, and Robert, the bouncer, is too.

"Holy crap! What the hell? Betty, I'm going to need a stronger drink." I banged on the bar.

She winked. "Coming up, Rick." Chuckling, she added, "I agree. You're definitely going to need it. DB just came in."

Take a deep breath.

Taking the drink I was offered, I chugged it back and when DB came to stand beside me, I smiled.

One look at me and his eyes went wide in shock. "What the hell did you do, Rick? We've been worried about you. When the hell did this happen?" He took my face in his hands.

"Please, don't be upset with me. I made a mistake."

"You bet your ass you did."

DB give him a break. It was almost my birthday. Baron Samedi didn't have a choice.

DB's expression grew angry. "Elvis, he did have a choice. I bet the bone man did something to cause this." He turned his attention back to me. "And what did you have to give up to have Elvis placed inside you?"

"Nothing. I have to look for Selvis." I sipped my drink unapologetically.

RICK THE DEAD CREOLE CLUB

"Yes, but you must have to give him something." His tone was full of disgust.

"If I fail, he gets to pick my punishment."

DB started to chuckle. "Oh, and you will fail. He'll make sure of that."

I watched as he stomped away.

You need to go after him.

"After I finish my drink," I stubbornly said.

Fine, but the longer you wait, the longer he must feel hurt.

Quickly slugging back the rest of my drink, I slid the glass to Betty.

"Hey, Robin, I think I need to go speak with DB and see what's wrong with him." I stood up from my stool. "I know I'll see you around again, right?" I asked for confirmation. When he nodded, I left and headed toward DB's office.

STANDING OUTSIDE HIS DOOR, I took a deep breath. "What do I say to him?

Start with I'm sorry. You know deep down that's why he's mad.

"I know." Instantly feeling defeated that I had hurt the one person who was a father figure to me, I knocked on the door. Silence followed, so, I knocked again. I waited patiently and when I received no answer, I went to leave. Finally, he said, "Come in.

Turning the knob, I opened the door and slowly walked inside. "Hey, big boss man. Can I say how sorry I am>"

He glanced up at me from over his laptop, his glasses slid down his nose. "Sit," he instructed.

I sat and waited for him to speak.

"Rick, how did this happen?" He sternly asked, not bothering to pull his focus from his laptop.

"It was a mistake. One I regret, but I was mugged outside my house."

"And I'm sure *he* had everything to do with that. His tone was stilted.

DB, he felt he didn't have a choice. My birthday was coming, and you were otherwise occupied, Elvis said.

"Besides, DB, you're not my father." The moment the words came out I knew they stung, but I couldn't retract them no matter how horrible I felt. It broke my heart to see the hurt in his eyes.

Rick, now that was not called for, Elvis chastised.

But I ignored him. I had lost the love of my life, and everyone was treating me like a child.

"Do you know what you've gotten yourself into?" DB asked, closing his laptop, leaning back, and folding his arms over his chest.

I got angry and leaned forward in the chair.

Be careful with the words you choose, Elvis warned.

Of course, I ignored him and continued, my anger intensifying. "Did Aaron or Robin know what they were getting into? Will the others know what they will be getting into when they make their deal?"

"Touche." DB glared at me. "I just wish you would have stayed in your house."

"The bone man said my fate was dealt for me. It was no use."

"Maybe, but I could have been there with you when this happened." His tone softened as he removed his glasses and rubbed the bridge of his nose.

Give him a break. DB cares about you. He's hurt you didn't wait for him. He's also worried about you, you... uh... know.

I watched DB's expression and knew that he could hear

Elvis. "You can hear him, can't you?" I grinned, already knowing the answer.

He nodded.

"Can Aaron still hear him?" I paused, wondering if Robin could as well since he was dead. Then I asked, "Can Robin still hear him, too?"

"I think so. I know Robin couldn't speak to him in his head. He was so angry that he let his emotions control things.

Yes, so be careful not to let your emotions control you and you will be able to speak... uh to me...uh... like that.

"How do I accomplish that?" I asked, but something in the mirror over DB's shoulder caught my eye.

Standing, it called to me. I walked being pulled forward by an imaginary force. When I stood before it, I gasped.

"What's wrong?" DB asked.

"Looking at him in the mirror is much different than in the Underworld."

"What do you mean?"

"Well, when I stared into the mirror..." I stopped speaking and kept staring.

"Go on," DB prodded as he stood and came to stand behind me. "How did he look in the Underworld?" He sounded curious.

I couldn't stop staring into the mirror. Finally, DB nudged me. I blinked. "Oh sorry, he resembled a skeleton. It was creepy."

"How do you see him here?" He asked.

"I see him as the seventies Elvis from *That's the Way It Is*."

Oh, that was a good time.

"Yes, I've watched that movie so many times I think I wore out my DVD. Now I have it streaming."

What's that? Elvis asked in wonderment.

I turned away from the mirror and stared at DB. "We have so much to teach him."

"Yes, but first we need to discuss your deal with the bone man. How do you plan on not failing?"

Walking back around his desk, I slumped in the chair in defeat. "I have no idea."

"Tell me what else you discussed."

I feared telling him about seeing Josephine. He might tell me not to go, and I desperately wanted to see her one last time. "There was not much more, DB."

I lied.

Chorus
Baron Samedi

After Elvis and Rick had been sent back topside, I sat behind my desk contemplating the conversation I'd had with my wife. There was no way in the Underworld I would let her in on all my fun, and still I sensed she had someone lurking around. And I was damned sure I was going to find out who it was.

Erik came in and sat in his chair. "Hey, I know what will take your mind off of everything going on here."

"What?" I inquired of my right-hand man.

Skeley interrupted us. "You can tell us the story of how yours truly was created," he squealed with glee.

Erik rolled his eyes and covered his ear holes.

"That might work." Standing, I went over to Skeley. "Please try to limit your screams. You know how it bothers Erik."

"That's what makes it fun," he whispered as his head came out of the painting and turned into a dial.

I spun it and Skeley screamed but I managed to remove the book with limited altercations. Walking back to my desk, I saw all the little skeletons sitting in formation waiting for me to tell the story of Skeley's creation.

"It looks like everyone's ready." I put the heavy book down on the desk with a thud, sat, opened the book, and carefully began to flip the pages.

"Hurry! Hurry!" Skeley screeched impatiently.

I glared over at the painting. "Give me some time."

Finally, I came to his creation story. Spreading my gloved hand over the crisp pages, I remembered everything like it was yesterday.

"Are you going to share with us?" Skeley pouted from his painting.

Looking up, I warned, "You must be patient."

"I'm trying my best but you're making it rather difficult by not reading my story RIGHT NOW!" He screamed again, which only caused Erik to cover his ears and sigh in exasperation.

"Skeley, we must be patient." I flipped through the book and finally came to his story. "Look, here it is."

"Thank God," he drawled out.

"Hey, what did I tell you about using that language here?"

"I'm sorry. Now, can we please get to my story?"

"Fine."

The little skeletons moved closer. Some even flopped onto their bellies and kicked their legs in the air.

"Here's the story of how our elusive Skeley was created." Little One crawled closer to me and curled up in the crook of my arm. I patted her head then started to read from the book.

. . .

An unknown artist passed away in the early 1800's. When his soul left his body I took it to the seventh gate. He was devastated that he hadn't made his mark in the world. So, I told him, "I'll give you a chance to do something spectacular."

"What would that be?" He asked me.

"I have a special project, and I think only someone of your caliber can do it," I told him.

He was thrilled, to say the least, and was ecstatic to remain here for some time to finish Skeley, although he didn't know the consequences of staying past his time.

"You didn't tell him what would happen to him?" Gasped Erik.

"Why would I? If I had, I would not have Skeley," I snickered.

"Can we get back to little ole me?" Skeley whined.

"Oh, of course." I grinned and smoothed out the page I was reading.

I set him up close to the seventh gate to keep an eye on him. I gave him brushes, paint, and a canvas so he could create. It took him only seven months to create what I asked of him. One day as he was painting, he called to me. I could hear his desperate cries from my office. In a flash, I appeared before him. "What is it?"

With a stroke of his brush, he stepped back and looked at me. "What is the meaning of this?"

"What do you mean?" I asked in faux concern.

Taking his brush, he swept it across the canvas and the scene changed. Then, as if in slow motion, we both watched as it moved to previous scenes he had painted.

Chuckling loudly, I caused an echo which made the walls shake, rattle, and roll. The structures encasing the long-past dead shattered into a million pieces and their skeletal arms broke free reaching out to us.

"It seems as if the magic of the underworld has seeped into your painting." I nonchalantly explained. "Now, can you paint a dial of a safe in the middle for me, please?"

Gawking at me, his expression was full of confusion, but he shrugged his shoulders, and said "I can do that."

I stood back leaning against the now silent wall and watched as he painted a perfectly round dial with roman numerals in perfect circular formation. "Ahh perfect." I reflected on what I looked upon. "What else is needed?" I wondered tapping a finger to my chin.

The painter stared at me waiting for his next direction.

"Aha!" I exclaimed. "Paint me a skeleton around the dial, and he obliged, gasping loudly when a skeleton face appeared followed by little skeleton legs and arms.

"WHAT HAPPENED TO THE ARTIST?" Erik asked curiously, interrupting.

"Ahh, when he found out that he was destined to remain in the Underworld forever, he grew angry at my trickery and threatened to throw Skeley into the Bayou of Lost Souls."

"No way!" Skeley squawked, before grumpily adding, "Well, hell, I dodged a bullet, didn't I?" Skeley plopped down on the raft in the river of his painting. "I wonder what would have happened if I ended up in the Bayou of Lost Souls?"

"It would be quiet in here," Erik sarcastically replied.

Ignoring both, I glanced back to the book. Taking my gloved hand, my fingers swept the yellowed pages and I began to read again.

. . .

As the artist grew angrier, he became disgruntled. On multiple occasions, he tried to destroy the painting. However, since the magic of the Underworld was incorporated inside of Skeley, the artist could do no harm. In the end, like any damaged soul, he walked the tunnels for a decade. It was a sad day indeed when I watched him end his torture by throwing himself into the Bayou of Lost Souls.

Erik gulped loudly. "He's one of the souls?"

"Yes, he is." I closed the book carefully then strummed my fingers on the leather cover. After waiting enough time, knowing the inevitable was about to happen. I sighed but resigned myself and stood, walking over to Skeley.

He winked at me, put his hands on his hips. "What are you waiting for boss man?"

He knew exactly what I was waiting for. I was tiring of his screaming every time I turned him. Though that I had no control over. That was the painters doing, but I had left that out of the story. When the artist jumped his scream echoed and bounced off the painting. But I digress nothing I could do now but return the book to the safe where it belonged and go through the entire torturous endeavor.

The second I closed the door though a squeal pierced my nonexistent ears then I saw Skeley run off with the book.

Way Down
Rick

I wasn't a hundred percent sure DB believed me. Thankfully, I was saved by the ringing of my cell phone. Sliding the green button, I answered while DB sat there quietly.

"Yes, yes," I replied to the person on the phone. "We'll be there the day after next. Thank you," I replied then disconnected the call.

"Who was that?" DB asked as soon as I shoved my phone back into my pocket.

I pinched my lips together, and looked him in the eye. "That was Josephine's mother. She called to tell me the time and place of the funeral."

"Good. We'll be there with you,". he adamantly replied. "Now, why don't you get some rest? I have some work to do."

As I got up to leave, he stopped me. "Please, don't do something stupid and go to Shreveport without us."

Giving him a smirk, I scoffed, "Kind of difficult since my keys were stolen, and I haven't had a chance to replace them.'"

"Oh, right," he replied.

Rick, give him a break. He's having a hard time, Elvis told me as I left DB's office.

"Right," I sarcastically huffed.

Remember, he cares about you. So, he worries about your wellbeing.

I knew what Elvis said was the truth. Yet, I was the one that had lost the love of my life.

Two Days later

Facing the black and white trimmed coffin, the American flag that had once covered it had been folded. It sat in her mother's lap as tears streamed down her face.

I couldn't move. I just stood there staring at the casket as they lowered it into the ground. My breath trembled. For a millisecond, I considered jumping in after it, but would good would that do? Josephine was dead.

DB stood beside me, but remained silent, placing a comforting hand on my shoulder for just a few moments. Before I knew it, all my friends stood beside me in a line, witnessing the love of my life sinking deep into the ground.

Aaron nudged me. "Don't look now, but Zerrin is standing behind us."

Barely turning around, I wondered what in the world he was doing there. We hadn't spoken since he'd left with Kingston.

"Ignore him," DB instructed.

"I can't. I want to know why he's here." Ignoring him, I was just about to make my way to the tree where Zerrin Snow stood, when something caught my eye. The skeletal man was leaning against a tomb smiling at me. Tipping his hat, he waved for me to come to him.

"Damn, what the hell is he doing here?" I wondered out loud.

DB swung his head around to see who I was talking about.

"Who?" Jacob and Aaron asked in unison. Turning their heads to see who I was talking about, they spat, "Oh, shit! What is he doing here?"

"Rick, you stay here. I'm going to see what he wants." DB patted me on the shoulder and started to leave.

"No, DB, I've got this."

"If you need us, you holler." Jess said as I walked away.

My thoughts of Zerrin disappeared at the site of Baron Samedi waiting for me. As I left, Jacob, Jess, and the others asked what the skeletal man wanted at Josephine's funeral. Thankfully, Aaron told them not to worry.

Be careful, Elvis warned as we walked toward the loa of the dead.

Stalking to the dilapidated tomb stone where he stood, I asked, "What are you doing here? You're far from home, aren't you?" I sneered getting a little too comfortable for his liking. I shuddered when his eyes turned black for a millisecond.

For a second time, he tipped his hat at me. "I'm here to take you to say goodbye to your sweet Josephine." He said in a sing song voice.

"Wait. Is it that time?" I gasped in amazement. "How is that possible?"

"We actually don't have that much time." He grinned widely.

I glanced over my shoulder at my friends still standing by the massive hole in the ground. Staring in my direction, they stood in a protective stance.

Glancing at the tree where Zerrin had been standing, I was shocked to see he was no longer there.

Good riddance, he must have left.

DB glared in our direction, but I ignored him. Turning back to face the skeletal man, I asked, "What do I need to do?"

He threw his head back, he laughed. "Not much, just hold my hand." I was just about to take ahold of his outstretched hand, but before I could, DB was standing beside me.

"What the hell is going on here?" He forcefully demanded.

The skeletal man's expression was instantly full of rage. "DB, this does not concern you."

"If it pertains to my tributes, I'd say it does," DB contradicted him, standing his ground. Sliding his feet shoulder-width apart, he grew to be almost as tall as the bone man.

How did he do that? Normally, DB stood about six-foot-tall and Baron Samedi towered over him by at least two feet.

"DB, look man, let me handle this please," I begged.

"Fine, but don't trust him," he snapped, turning around and walking back to the others while keeping a watchful eye on me.

Turning back to Baron Samedi, I got right back to business. "So, how do we do this?"

"Just grab my hand." He chuckled. "It's quicker that way."

As soon as my fingers touched him, DB roared, "No?" as I disappeared.

When the world finally stopped spinning, I stood in a very dark place. Off to my left was a strange body of water. Hundreds of souls bobbed up and down, screaming and wailing so loudly that I covered my ears, because the pain was deafening.

"What is this?"

"Those are the souls of the people that never crossed over."

I haven't been here, Elvis exclaimed. *This isn't good.*

"Why didn't they cross over?" I suspiciously inquired.

Tapping a bony finger to his lips, he readily explained, "They either did not have the coin to take the boat over or something caused them to not cross."

Glancing down, I saw an opaque hand reaching for me. Jumping out the way just in time, I yelped, "What the hell?"

He ignored me and asked. "Are you ready, Mr. Miceli?"

I nodded.

Rick, are you sure about this? Elvis asked but I ignored him.

"Good. She should be here soon. That is if she has not gotten lost coming through the gates."

"What do you mean if she hasn't gotten lost?"

He didn't answer. Instead, he stood in the middle of the wharf watching the souls as they reached for him and begged for rest.

"How much longer do we have to wait?" I asked impatiently.

"Rick, down here time doesn't matter."

"But wait, you said we didn't have much time." I was confused.

He danced around and, he lyrically answered, "I meant, we did not have much time to get here to meet her. If she arrived while I was getting you, we could have missed her. In that case, she would have been wandering around here for an eternity. We would not want that, now, do we?"

Nodding in agreement, I worried the bone man was playing with me.

Then I saw her—my Josephine. She looked frightened as she neared the wharf. I couldn't move. My feet were planted as if I was wearing cement boots.

"Why don't you go to her?" Baron Samedi slapped me on the back.

I still couldn't move. I tried. I honestly tried, but I was stuck.

The closer she came, the more my breath caught in my throat, traveling down to my stomach. Her long brown hair flowed around past her shoulders. The moment our eyes met, a look of sadness crossed her beautiful face.

"Rick, what are you doing here? Wait! Where am I?"

Finally managing to make myself move, I met her halfway. Taking her in my arms, I inhaled the sweet scent of jasmine. Pulling back from her, I looked at her face, trying not to frighten her.

"Josephine, you're dead. And to answer your other question, you're in the Underworld. Baron Samedi will take you where you need to go."

She latched onto me, her voice was muffled as she spoke against my neck. "Wait! Are you dead, too?" Panicking, she trembled in my arms.

Pulling her closer and holding her tighter, I tried to comfort the woman I loved. "No, Josephine. I'm not dead. I was just given the opportunity to tell you goodbye."

"Oh, Rick. I'm so sorry for the let..."

"Ahem," the bone man interrupted us. "I am so sorry, but time is up. I need to take her to her final destination."

"Can I go with you?" I asked, trying my best to stall him.

"Absolutely not." He shook his head vehemently. "I already caused chaos by bringing you here."

"Wait! What the hell?" I exclaimed angrily. "Did you trick me?"

A smile curved his bony face, but just as quickly as it had appeared–it was gone. "We will discuss this when I get back. Rest assured, we have much to discuss." Stepping onto the alligator-shaped boat that had just arrived, he held out a gloved hand to Josephine. "Do you have coin for the ride?" He asked.

Shit Rick, I told you not to trust him, Elvis admonished.

I couldn't pay attention to him. I needed to make sure Josephine had a coin.

Looking from me to Baron Samedi with a combined expression of fear and panic etched across her beautiful face, her eyes grew wide. She was terrified,

My heart skipped a beat and my stomach rolled. I couldn't have her live for all eternity in the murky waters below me. Digging into the pockets of my jeans, I was surprised to find a coin inside. Pulling it out, I placed it in the palm of her hand.

Closing her hand tightly over the currency, I smiled, "Here." Then I gave her one last kiss.

"Are you sure? I mean after...what...I," She stuttered.

"I'm sure." I placed a finger to her lips. "You need to go to your final resting place."

She nodded and I watched as she passed the coin to Baron Samedi. Taking his outstretched hand, she stepped onto the boat. He eyed the coin then shoved it in his breast pocket. "Ahh, what a sacrifice. It's kind of you to offer her coin after what she..." He stopped short and shook his head. "Never mind.

"What the hell are you talking about?"

"Rick, you stay here. I will be back soon and then we will talk." His smirk sent chills up and down my spine.

Chorus
Baron Samedi

R ick was sitting on the wharf with his legs pulled tightly up to his chest when I returned. Some of the souls still reached for him, but he ignored them.

He was deep in thought. I assumed he was thinking about the woman I had sent to her final place. Pulling the boat next to the wooden wharf, it slammed against a soul. Honestly, it should have gotten out of the way. It screeched in protest, but I paid no mind as I stepped out of the boat.

"Rick, Josephine is where she's supposed to be," I assured him as the soles of my boots thudded on the wooden wharf.

Barely looking up, he sadly asked, "Did it hurt?"

Shrugging, I continued past him, sighing, "I have no idea."

"What were you talking about when you took her away?"

"Oh, that's best explained at another time."

"What do you mean?"

"It means, I do not have time to talk about it now. Best follow me," I ordered, looking over my shoulder for a second.

A stray soul managed to climb on the pier and grab his leg just as he stood. He tried in vain to shake it off, but somehow, it climbed on top of him, trying to drag him into the Bayou of Lost Souls.

Rick screamed, causing me to turn around and scoffed loudly, "Damn it all to hell!"

Stomping back to him, I caught him just mere minutes before he was lost forever. Picking him up by the collar, he dangled just inches above the murky water.

"Follow me when I tell you," I snapped, plopping him back onto the wharf. "Now, let's go. They can smell blood."

Walking side by side, I knew Rick was nervous about what was going to happen to him. After a few moments, he stopped and turned to me. "Baron Samedi, why did you trick me?"

I chuckled loudly. "Because I can, Rick. Because I can."

"So, what is going to happen to me?"

Stopping in my tracks, I pondered his question. "Well, when a human doesn't go through the gates, the correct way–as you did–a demon goes topside to wreak havoc. So, Mr. Maceli, this is your decision, your sacrifice to the Underworld to calm her."

"What do you want?"

I tapped my chin with a bony, gloved finger. "Usually, I require a soul, but since you have a soul inside you, I'll do you a solid and remove part of yours."

He gasped loudly, and fell into the brick wall behind him, waking the inhabitants inside. Hands frantically broke through the stone and mortar, trying to escape their slab prison.

"That's enough!" I bellowed. After a few moments, they quieted down. Rick stood silent, staring at me, his eyes wide with shock.

"Mr. Miceli, or would you rather me call you, Rick?"

Still pressed against the wall, he stammered, "Uh, yes, uh... Rick's fine." Finally pushing himself away from the barrier, he added, "What if I don't agree to give up part of my soul?"

I glared at him. He shrunk back in fear. I knew Elvis was speaking to him. I hoped he was warning him.

"Rick, you really don't want me to unleash anything topside. Your best bet is to take my deal, to let me remove part of your soul. Now, let's get back to my office and finish so I can get you back topside. You still have a job to do for me, don't you?"

Grinning at him, I turned. He shrunk back in fear. I could only assume my devilish smile scared him just a bit, but he followed me nonetheless as I traversed the dank, dark tunnels to my office. One of these days, the humans might learn to stop letting me trick them. At the thought, I shook my head, as I walked through the catacombs. "Nah, that's never going to happen. They follow their emotions instead of their heads."

Back in my office, I sat behind my desk, evilly tapping my fingers together. How I was going to pull this off? I mean Elvis and Selvis were a total accident on my part. What I was about to do would be deliberate. I had to do it correctly or Rick would be messed up or worse.

I shuddered in sheer delight as the corners of my lips tugged upwards. Looking up, I was surprised. For a split second, I had forgotten my guest. He was still standing in the door of my office.

"Rick, come on in."

"What's got him so scared?" Skeley piped up from across the room.

Getting to my feet, I came from behind the desk. "Oh, nothing but a little taking of half his soul."

"What?" Skeley screeched.

"Oh, please don't act like that."

"Yeah, but didn't you get in trouble the last time you did that?" He asked, his voice a few octaves too high.

Rolling my eyes, I sat on the edge of my desk, crossing one leg over the other. Waving Rick inside, I coaxed him into the room. Begrudgingly, he sat in the chair in front of me.

"So, Mr. Boss man, how do you presume to manage this task?" Skeley asked.

Ignoring his insolence, I walked behind my desk where the box of cigars and an almost empty rum bottle sat. Opening the box, I pulled out a cigar, quickly clipping off the end and lighting it. Taking a quick puff, I then turned. Just as I did, I caught sight of the rum bottle again.

Grabbing it, I walked back around the desk and returned to my place on the edge. I grinned at the man in front of me. He sat there as if his whole world had been lost.

I almost felt sorry for him. Almost!

"Can we get this over with?"

"I wouldn't be in such a hurry, Rick."

"What else do I have to do? Where else do I have to go?" He incoherently mumbled.

"So, let's get this done." Popping the cork off the rum bottle, I held it in front of him. "This might hurt some. I've never purposefully done this before." I grinned.

"What the hell?" He sputtered.

"Shhh..." Leaning forward, I placed a gloved finger to his lips, saying the spell I'd prepared.

. . .

DEEP in the underworld
    I split this soul in two.
    In my hand it swirled
    Its cause to pay a debt
    But it needed a home.
    Found an old rum bottle.
    So, it couldn't roam.
    Now it's locked up safe.

Burning Love
Rick

           The pain of having my soul ripped in half was indescribable. I wanted to scream, but when I tried nothing came out. Elvis spoke in my head trying his best to comfort me, but it wasn't helping. I wished I'd listened to DB and hadn't come to see Josephine.

As the pain started to dissipate, I realized I happy that I got to see her one last time. The pain was somehow worth it.

Are you all right Rick? Elvis asked as I lay there breathing heavily.

In the process of having part of my soul ripped from me, I'd slipped from the chair onto the floor. Staring up at the ceiling of the loa's office, I watched the dancing skeleton.

I thought they were hallucinations. I had no idea if they were a figment of my imagination caused by the immense pain I'd suffered, or if they truly existed.

RICK THE DEAD CREOLE CLUB

As I lay on the cold dirt floor, a memory of my Josephine came to me like the flood after a hurricane"

"COME ON, Rick, we're going to be late," my buddy Zerrin called to me.

We had a double date with Josephine and one of her friends. Unbeknownst to me, Zerrin was thrilled because he'd had his eye on one of the pretty ladies. He was jumping at the bit, and I was taking my time because I wanted everything to be perfect.

"All right, all right." I dragged a hand down the front of my pants smoothing them and made sure my shirt looked good. Why the hell was I so nervous? Walking out, I witnessed Zerrin pacing back and forth. It looked like he was as anxious as I was.

"Come on," I said, grabbing my keys. "Let's go pick up the girls."

THE DRIVE to the base took a while, but once we arrived, they were waiting. As they hopped inside, I faced Josephine. Her beauty still astounded me. I had no idea how I was so lucky.

"Where do you want to go?" I asked.

A sly grin curved her kissable lips. "I know it's a little cheesy, but can we act like we are in an Elvis movie and go to Rudesheimer Germany and ride the actual cable cars they used in the movie? And can you two sing to us? Oh, and afterwards, we'll get strudel. It only takes about an hour to get there."

"Do you girls have the time to be away that long?"

Josephine nodded. "We do. Don't we, Nina?"

"Zerrin, you up for a road trip?"

"I sure am," he said, settling comfortably in the back seat with his arm around Nina.

"Then it's settled. Let's go to ride the cable cars," I happily agreed, starting the car.

WHEN WE ARRIVED at our destination, it was the most beautiful place I'd ever seen, but still not as beautiful as the woman standing beside me. Zerrin and I helped the ladies onto the cable cars and as soon as we were high up in the air they looked at us and smiled.

With the girls on the opposite side, we smiled at each other, and we recreated the iconic scene by singing a Pocket Full of Rainbows. The soft melody floated on the air around us, following as our cable car balanced on the wire high above the mountains.

Gently reaching for Josephine's hand, I sang to only her. For a moment, it felt as if we were the only two in the world, high above everything and everyone, flying in the sky.

Looking into her blue eyes, I could see only her. The touch of her skin against mine sealed our connection. I was so enthralled, that I didn't even realize when the ride ended. I was caught up in only her.

AWAKENED from the sweetest memory I'd ever had by searing pain, I realized it had only been a dream. Staring up into the face of Baron Samed, I wanted off the cold, dirty floor.

Rick, I don't feel like there is any difference in you. Elvis tried to comfort me.

But I did feel different. A part of me had been ripped away. The bone man lied to me. It hurt like hell, but honestly even though the pain was still unbearable, I knew deep down I would do it again, if just to see Josephine one last time.

And DB. Oh crap, when he found out, he was going to be so pissed. But what the hell did I care.?

But Rick, you do care, Elvis corrected, trying to make me feel guilty.

Suddenly, Baron Samedi's gloved hand helped me off the floor. Sitting me upright in the chair, he said with an eerier smile, "There, that has to feel better."

I remained seated for a few minutes, getting my bearings. Looking around, I blinked. The room was just as I'd remembered from the last time.

"Are you ready to return topside?" The bone man asked.

I barely nodded. "I think so," I barely squeaked out my reply.

Leaning in closer, he intently inquired, "Are you sure? You must be sure. I can't have you looking like death when I return you."

I tried to hold in my laughter I failed. Instead, I said. "Well, that'll be hard now, won't it? I'm practically dead."

Flaring at he, he chose not to reciprocate. Getting to the point, he reminded, "Anyway, don't forget to search for Selvis. You have until the anniversary of the death of your companion.

"I have a question before I go topside. How do I live with half a soul?"

Of course, as usual, there was no answer. I was simply whisked away.

Chorus
Baron Samedi

After I returned Rick and Elvis, minus half a soul, topside, I stared at the rum bottle. What was left of the opaque and shimmery spirit floated around the bottom of the amber, glass bottle. It looked at me and bounced off the side of the glass begging to be let out.

"Look at the little guy," cooed Skeley. "He's drinking what's left."

I shook the bottle then tapped it. "Stop that. I don't need you drunk."

The half soul stared at me, then stuck out his tongue. I ignored him and turned my attention to Skeley.

"Are you going protect him?" I held the glass container close to my chest. The inhabitant bumped against the sides.

He placed a hand over his chest, Skeley sing-song, "Isn't that what I was made for?"

"That it is, but this is here is very important." Without waiting for a reply, I demanded, "Now, assume the position."

WHEN HE DID, I spun the dial, and he screamed. Stopping at the correct number, I glared at him. The half soul cowered in the bottom of his new home as possible.

"Skeley, look! You've scared your new guest."

He rolled his eyes from his dial. "Puhlease. I did no such thing," he whined.

Right in the middle of putting our new guest in Skeley, Erik sauntered into my office. "Why the hell are you opening him? I thought you already had a contract?" He sighed, plopping down in his chair.

"I have a new friend staying with me," Skeley replied with glee.

"What!" Erik spun in his chair with his phone still in his hand. "What is the silly painting talking about?" Jumping to his feet, he stalked toward us.

I grimaced at my second in command. I just wanted to finish opening Skeley and place the rum bottle containing half of Rick's soul inside.

Anything That's Part of You
Rick

I stood on the street where Baron Samedi left me. Shuddering, I tried my best to shake off the feeling that I was somehow different.

I can't believe you did that.

"Did what?" I pretended to not know what Elvis was talking about.

Let the bone man take half your soul.

"What were my choices?"

That's true. You make a fine point.

"Wouldn't you have done the same thing to see a loved one for the last time?"

Elvis was quiet for a moment then he spoke. *Yeah, you're right. I would have done the same thing if the love of my life died before me.*

"We do crazy things for love," I said, walking down the sidewalk. The sky darkened, causing the gas lanterns above me to flicker to life. The club would be opening soon.

What do you think DB is going to say when he finds out?" Elvis asked.

"How do you know he'll find out?"

A loud, booming laugh echoed inside my skull, forcing me to my knees. When Elvis finally stopped, I slowly let go off my temples. Thankfully, he tone was softer. *You know one look at you and he's going to know.*

"Damn it, you're right." Dragging myself up from the ground, I noticed Robert wasn't manning the club door. I quickly snuck inside and waved at Betty who was behind the bar talking to Robin. The club was empty of our regulars and I immediately knew why Robert wasn't manning the door. I had managed to miss the black wreath hanging on it signaling a death. "Damn time does move differently down there?" I mumbled under my breath. I looked around and saw the tables laden with food and desserts I assumed from the Clambake and The Shake Pinch and Roll.

Yeah it does.

Stopping, to chat with Robin and Betty, "hey where is every...?" But before I could finish.

"Whoa, what the hell happened to you?" Robin asked, peering closer at my face.

Pulling away from his interrogation, I asked, "What do you mean?" Instantly, I pretended not to know what he was talking about.

Turning around on the barstool to face me, he glared. "Cut the crap Rick! You only have a half a soul in your body."

"Shh." I returned his glare. "I don't need the whole club to hear."

Moving to face Betty, who frowned at us, he grumbled, "No, you mean you don't want DB to find out."

That's what I told him, Elvis snickered.

Robin shook his head as Aaron walked up to us. "Hey it's about time you showed up." He said with one of Larisa's treats in his hands.

"Wait till you get a load of what Rick has been up to," Robin scoffed, putting his glass to his lips.

Stopping mid-smile, Aaron yelped dropping the treat on the bar, "What the fuck Rick?" Taking my face in his hands, he peered closely into my eyes.

I tried to pull it from his grasp but to no avail.

"Hold still. I'm trying to see if what I'm seeing is true." With his face was mere inches from mine, he confirmed, "Yes, I see Elvis and half of your soul."

Tugging free of his hold on my face, I scowled.

"Don't give me that look, Aaron snapped. "What the fuck did you do? We've been worried about you since you disappeared from Josephine's funeral."

"How long was I gone?"

He shook his head. "Don't change the subject." Another shake of his head and he went on, "To answer your question, you've been gone two days."

"But what about all this food?" I waved my hand.

"We've been waiting for you to return. Leaning in, he practically demanded, "Now, answer my fucking question. What did you do to lose part of your soul?"

Betty slid a drink my way. "I think you're going to need one of these." She smiled creepily.

"Thanks." I took it, slugging it down in one gulp.

Pulling up one of the barstools, Aaron waited patiently for

me to tell my story. Hitting my glass on the bar, I indicated that I needed another drink before I was ready.

Stop delaying the inevitable, Elvis chastised me.

"Fine.," I grumbled, chugging the second drink Betty slid my way.

Tossing her towel over her shoulder, she leaned her skeletal elbows against the bar. Robin entwined his fingers with hers, but I shook my head as Aaron stared at me, wanting me to speak.

When I started talking, they hung on to every word as I told them everything that happened in the Underworld. After I'd finished, Aaron sat there slack jawed and Betty leaned back from the bar, quickly placing three drinks in front of us.

"Damn, you all need one of these."

I think Aaron is in shock, Elvis said as we stared at him sitting there.

Waiting for him to speak took longer than I expected, but then he spoke. "Rick, you know DB is not going to be happy about this."

"I'm not going to be happy about what?" A voice said from behind us.

I didn't dare turn around, not from fear but from not wanting to deal with his anger. I had dealt with enough.

"Aaron can you go let the others that Rick has returned," DB instructed.

"Sure, boss man," he said, slipping from the barstool without looking at me.

Chorus
Baron Samedi

After Skeley finished screaming, I placed the rum bottle containing half of Rick's soul inside the safe. Walking to my desk, I leaned on edge and wondered why things could not be easier. At least, hopefully, Rick would soon find Selvis and he would be in my grasp.

"Ahh," I sighed in relief and sat in my chair.

Erik ran in. He was completely out of breath.

"What in the world is wrong with you?" I asked, taking a cigar from my cypress cigar box.

Relaxing in the wingback chair, I propped my feet on my desk, oblivious to Erik's issues. I cut the tip off the cigar and lit it. Inhaling deeply, I watched the nerdy skeleton plop into the chair in front of my desk.

"Erik, pray tell, what is wrong with you?" I nonchalantly repeated my question.

He did not answer right away. Instead, he huffed and puffed, still trying to catch his breath.

Waiting with as much patience as I could muster, I continued to blow little skeleton smoke rings, killing time until he was ready to explain his tizzy. I peered around my second in command, and looked for Skeley.

He was nowhere in sight. Thank goodness for small miracles. No need for the peanut gallery tonight.

"Lawson and I... A clue to where Selvis might be... but then..." He paused, still wheezing.

"Then what? Go on," I insisted.

His eyes went wide. "I can't. It's about your wife."

Instantly sitting up straight, I pulled my legs from the desk. My boots scraped across the cypress wood, completely ignoring the pesky nail sticking out from the wood.

One of the little skeletons peeked from their hiding spot, quickly ducking back inside. "What the hell has she done?" I growled.

"She has Lawson. She said he was a spy." Another huff and one more puff, and he added, "But that's not all boss man."

"What more could there be?"

Trembling at my question, his knees clacked together like two drumsticks. "I... uh... swear that she's working with someone."

Shaking my head, I caused the skeletons atop my hat to shift unsteadily. "That, my dear Erik, is not possible."

"But...but..." He stuttered.

"Look, you sit and calm yourself. I will go rescue Lawson from the evil clutches of my dear wifey."

"Oh, shit, what's happening?" Skeley appeared, late to the party.

"I will let Erik fill you in when he stops hyperventilating

from his recent run in with my wife," I grumbled, exiting my office.

Tᴇɴ ᴍɪɴᴜᴛᴇꜱ later

Sᴛᴀʟᴋɪɴɢ ᴛʜʀᴏᴜɢʜ ᴛʜᴇ ᴛᴜɴɴᴇʟꜱ, I made my way toward my wife's abode. Stopping short of her door, I heard laughter followed by screams and the soft melody from her favorite album *Skulls! Skulls! Skulls!*

The music emanated from somewhere in the walls, but didn't stop me from barging into the room.

> *Skulls, are buried*
> *Skulls in the ground*
> *You'll find them in your nightmares Whoa, whoa whoa*
> *Skulls in your dreams*

"Wᴇʟʟ, well, what do we have here?" I asked, seeing poor Lawson sitting in the middle of at least four other loa.

It was a sad scene. They were placing tarantulas all over him and he was screaming.

Through it all, the soft melody played as he continued to scream.

> *Skulls can hear your screams*
> *They're terrifying, Damn I could Shriek*

*I'm just the wife of the loa
And I can't stop dreamin'*

*Skulls bobbin in the water
Skulls in tunnel walls
They'll scare ya till
ya scream Whoa whoa whoa
Skulls red and bloody
Skulls white and chalky
But be careful or you'll
Be the next hiding in your dreams whoa whoa who*

MAMAN BRIDGITTE QUICKLY STOOD, trying to hide her angry expression. "Dear husband, what brings you to my place?" Her tone was sugary sweet as the familiar chorus played.

*I'm just the wife of the loa
And I can't stop dreamin'
skulls skulls skulls*

*And when I see a skull the urge to pick it up
And squeeze, squeezing
Squeeze, squeezing
Is the most appeasing.
Feeling because it's death in my hand*

. . .

Skulls lying about
Skulls scattered around
As a fine decoration whoa whoa whoa
Skulls on the walls
Skulls in the halls
I'm ready to go a decoratin'

I'm just the wife of the loa
And I can't stop dreamin'
skulls skulls skulls

COCKING A BROW, I waited for the song to end. "I heard you had one of my skeletons here."

"Oh, is he one of yours?" she draped an arm over Lawson, but he tried to move away from her with no such luck. "I had no idea." Her tone was again sickly sweet, a tell-tale sign she was lying.

I eyed her. "Now, you know that is not true."

A huge tarantula crawled across Lawson's face, he continued to scream in agony as it almost entered his mouth. I covered my nonexistent ears. Leaning on my staff I turned to Erzulie Freda, I politely asked, "Ma'am, would you please stop that while I speak with my wife? I cannot hear myself talk with all the screeching."

I was glad Erik was not here. He would not have been able to stand the shrieking.

Erzulie Freda picked up the tarantula from Lawson. Remnants of sweat dripped down his faces as he heaved a sigh of relief. Then I turned to face my angry wife.

"Samedi, why do you come in here and make demands of my friends?"

"Wife. why are you torturing one of mine?"

"I told you I did not know he was."

Sucking on my teeth, I tried a different approach. "Then why is he deserving of such torture?"

She grinned wide. "He was in here..." She waved her arms around. ..."digging through my stuff..." She enunciated those words to make a point.

"I think you are wrong. My Lawson would not do such a thing."

Her eyes turned black. "You call me a liar?"

"I did not call you a liar. I simply think you may be mistaken." Trying to backpedal before I found myself with a tarantula on me, I stood perfectly still.

My wife eyed me suspiciously. "What is this about Samedi? What is he to you?"

Taking her in my arms, I cooed, "He is nothing to me, just a lackey, but why waste perfectly good tarantulas on him

Nuzzling my neck, she murmured. "You are right. But if I see him snooping around here again, I will do worse to him." Leaning back, she looked up at me as her smile curved upward, making her face eerily macabre. It was the reason I fell in love with her.

Pushing back from her, I glared. Suddenly, I sensed someone, or something, watching us. It was not the four female loas sitting in the room.

I shuddered as a chill ran down my spine. "Fine. Now let him go," I demanded.

Nodding to Erzulie Freda, and the others, the female loas let the snakes go from Lawson's wrists and ankles. Slithering along the floor, away from his body, they simply disappeared.

I tried to sense what was in the room, but I could not. Whatever, or whoever, was deceiving me.

"I will see you later, dear wife."

"Yes, you will." She grinned.

Leaving my wife's place, Lawson practically ran ahead of me. Once we were a few tunnels away, he finally stopped. Crouching, his wheezing stopped as he finally slowed his breathing. "Baron Samedi, I can't spy for you anymore. It's too dangerous."

I remained silent for a few seconds then spoke. "What if I could promise to protect you?"

He looked up at me cocking a brow. "Can you really make that promise? Because short of a spell to hide me from your wife, I don't see how you could possibly keep your word."

"Well, let me work on that."

Doncha' Think It's Time
Rick

Aaron came back followed by VK, his wife and the others.

VK sat beside me and looked at me. "Hell I thought Aaron was pulling my leg." He said as he looked at me. "Damn you are going to be in so much trouble." He slapped his leg and spun around on the barstool accepting the drink Betty offered. "Rick, you know you are going to have to tell DB, right?" Aaron grinned.

"But do I?"

I agree. He's going to be mad if you don't offer the information first.

I sighed, knowing they were right. But I didn't have time to discuss it right now.

"Hey guys are we doing this?" Jess asked leaning against the bar.

"Doing what?" I wondered.

Aaron slapped me on the shoulder. "Well my friend after you disappeared Josephine's parents asked if we would do a benefit show for the army family's."

I looked at him. "And let me guess DB said yes."

He slapped me on the shoulder and said you got it brother. Now we need to all get ready. Because I think Jacob's mom just walked in with more food from the Clambake. But first let me go help Larisa with her baked goods." He dashed off in the direction of the door of the club.

I looked at the others and shrugged my shoulders.

AN HOUR later

WAITING IN THE DARK SHADOWS, I hoped that when I stepped onto the stage DB wouldn't notice until I could speak to him.

We watched as DB paced back and forth entertaining the audience.

"Ladies and Gentlemen, do you want to hear a joke?" He asked.

"Yes!" They cheered.

"A truck full of Vicks vapor rub just turned over on the highway." Pausing for dramatic effect, he perfectly dropped his punchline. "There's been no congestion for four hours."

The crowd erupted in a fit of laughter.

Looking over at us, a stage light shined right on me. His eyes went wide, but he instantly regained his composure.

Shit he knows, Elvis said.

"Yes, he does. What do I do?"

Talk to him when he comes off the stage.

But before I could, I glanced out into the crowded sea of faces. One stood out. It resembled the one taking up residence in my body. "Is that who I think it is?" I asked Elvis.

Yes.

Selvis sat at the bar beside Robin. They were talking. I had to know what they were discussing. As DB introduced Aaron, I took my leave.

Dashing from the stage, I made my way through the crowd. Just a few seconds shy of my destination, I was stopped by Kingston.

"Hey Rick, you got time to chat?"

Glancing over his shoulder, I watched as Elvis's twin sat conversing with my ghost friend.

"No, Kingston. I don't have time," I rudely responded.

You should talk to him. It looks as if he is having a hard time, Elvis said.

"I don't really care if he's going through a hard time. What if I lose Selvis?" I muttered through clenched teeth, so Kingston wouldn't hear me.

Selvis looks like he's deep in conversation with Robin. Maybe you'll have time to see what this one wants.

Taking a closer look at Kingston, I realized that Elvis was right, he did look ragged. His baseball cap sat skewed on his head, and he hadn't shaved in a week.

Shoving my hands in my pocket, I glared at Kingston. "What do you need?" I waited for his answer, keeping an eye on the bar to see when, and if, Selvis moved.

"First, I wanted to say I'm sorry to hear about your girl."

"Thanks."

"Second, do you think I have a chance of DB helping me with my club?"

Glancing back to the bar, Selvis was no longer there.

"Dammit! I have to go." Starting past him, I added, "Talk to DB yourself. That's between the two of you. "I ran off toward the bar. I placed a hand on Robin's shoulder, but it sunk inside like I'd dipped it into a bowl of water.

Remember he's a ghost, Elvis reminded me.

Turning around on the barstool, Robin smiled. "What's going on?"

Sitting down, I faced Betty as if I was talking to her. I didn't want the people to think I was crazy. "Were you talking to Selvis?" I asked, not turning to face him.

"Yes, do you know him?"

"I know of him. We need to get him back here."

"Why?"

Before I could answer, DB came to stand behind me. The air around stood still. "Rick, I think we need to talk."

"About what?" I asked, not turning around to face him.

"You know."

"What if I don't want to talk about it."

I think you are going to have to talk about it, Elvis urged me.

Sitting there, hunched over, I was a little terrified to turn around, but I finally did. DB glared at me.

"Why did you do that?"

"What do you mean?" I smirked.

"You know damn well what I'm talking about," He pointed at my face. "You're missing half your soul."

"Look, I did what I needed to do to say goodbye to Josephine."

Shaking his head, he walked away. "It'll be your funeral. I can't keep protecting you."

"Are you actually claiming you are? I hollered at his retreating figure.

Okay that was uncalled for.

Chorus

Baron Samedi

I RETURNED to my office minus Lawson. Letting him return back to his own place, I promised him I'd work on a spell to hide him from Bridgitte. I know he didn't believe me, but I would do it.

However, at the moment, something else was on my mind. I had sensed something, or someone, in my wife's abode. Nevertheless, it was hidden from me.

Erik was sitting in his chair when I walked in, but I paid him no mind. My attention was the thing in my wife's room. Walking around my second in command, I practically flopped into my own.

The claw feet scraped against the dirt floor. The annoying sound scared the two skeletons in the room, as well as the tiny ones in the desk who scurried from their hiding spots.

"What's wrong with you?" Erik asked.

I didn't answer him.

Erik looked over his shoulder at Skeley. Little one peeked out and crawled to me. I glanced down at her when she tapped me on the wrist. Her little soulful eyes spoke to me. As she patted me on the hand, I nodded very slightly indicating she could dance for me. Letting my head fall back against the purple wingback chair, I shut my eyes—but not before waving a hand to turn on the gramophone.

The album skipped to the song I wanted to play. The soothing melody of *Nightmares* pushed most of today's troubles aside as the tune played from the album.

> *Nightmares (nightmares, nightmares)*
> *May your dreams be filled with nightmares*
> *I'm the king of Voodoo*
> *So, I can share them all with you*

KEEPING my eyes closed as the music played, I knew the little skeletons were dancing. However, if I didn't watch her during the chorus, my favorite little one would be peeved.

> *In your bed, (your bed, your bed)*
> *Laying in your bed, (in your bed)*
> *Can't you see I'll keep you*
> *Safe in nightmare land too*

> *I have the power to make*
> *The nightmares come at night (at night)*
> *They keep coming*
> *But don't you worry*
> *They will give a big fright (big fright)*
> *And your fear is quite unbecoming*

. . .

As the song played, I found myself opening my eyes. It continued to calm me. The little skeletons made slinking rubber band movements and rhythmical dance moves. I wondered when they had found the time to learn such dance steps. I was amazed at their skill.

In my realm, (my realm, my realm)
Oh sweet, in my realm, (my realm)

I'll sing you a song, *so you'll fall asleep*

And the nightmares will come

I have the power to make
The nightmares come at night (at night)
They keep coming
But don't you worry
They will give a big fright (big fright)
And your fear is quite unbecoming

In my realm, (my realm, my realm)
Oh sweet, in my realm, (my realm)

I'll sing you a song, *so you'll fall asleep*

DIANA MARIE DUBOIS

And the nightmares will come
Nightmares will come, nightmares will come

WHEN THE SONG ended my mood was somewhat better, not hundred percent, but I'd take it.

Echoes of Love
Rick

Crawling into bed, I did not even bother removing my clothes. I sighed a deep breath, my body sunk into the soft mattress. The ends of the pillow curled around my head and enveloped me. I was out before my eyelids closed.

That's when the memory came to me in the form of a dream.

WAITING PATIENTLY at Louis Armstrong National airport with Robin and Zerrin, my right knee bounced uncontrollably as I sat in one of the uncomfortable orange plastic chairs. Zerrin put his hand on my leg.

"Stop it. There's no reason to be nervous." He grinned.

"I know but..."

Robin put a hand up to stop me midsentence. "No. No buts..."

"I can't help but be nervous. It's been a while since I've seen her."

I was stopped again, but this time it was because of the pretty brunette walking through the terminal. Both guys slapped me on the back as I held back the urge to run to her.

"Is that her?" Robin asked.

Pushing myself from the chair, I stuffed my hands into my pockets, hoping the material would wipe away the sweat. I shifted from one foot to the other as a new wave of nerves hit me in the chest. Josephine looked sexy as hell in a short blue dress and black combat boots.

Robin nudged me. "Hey man, what did you say she did again?"

"She's a warrant officer in the army and pilots a Blackhawk."

"Damn man, you are lucky, aren't you?"

I smiled at him, knowing he spoke the truth.

Josephine saw me and started to run.

I smiled at my boys.

"Go get her," they said in unison then doubled over in laughter.

Ignoring them, I sauntered to her. Stopping before her, I removed my hands from my pockets, scooped her in my arms, and spun her around. As she slid down my chest, I planted a long, overdue kiss on her lips.

"So, where can a girl get a bite to eat around here?" She grinned, lighting up her face.

When she saw Zerrin standing at the edge of the terminal, she asked, "Is that...?"

I nodded, grinning. "He insisted on coming with me to pick you up. He's only in town for a couple of days," I bragged, walking toward him.

"Pfftt," Zerrin scoffed. "He dragged me here because he wanted someone to drive."

"Ahem," Robin cleared his throat.

"Damn, I'm sorry, man. Josephine, I'd like to introduce you to my friend, Robin, he works with me at the My Way Club."

They shook hands and I grabbed her suitcase. "So, what would you like to do first?

"Can we get a bite to eat?"

"Sure, what are you in the mood for?"

"Something sweet." She laughed.

I placed an arm around her waist. "My baby always did have a sweet tooth. I know the perfect place."

With traffic and finding a place to park, it took us all but an hour to get to Chris's Sweet Treats Shoppe. I told Josephine she had to try the brownies that they were to die for. When we walked up, I noticed a for sale sign on the front door, but thank goodness the place was still open.

The bell tinkled as the four of us entered, alerting the owner, Chris to come out from the back. She smiled as the others found a table and I approached the counter to order.

She smiled. "Your usual, Rick?"

"Yes, I want my girl to taste your brownies."

"I'll throw in a bit of Chantilly cake for her as well. I just made some."

"Thanks."

"So you're selling the place?"

She nodded. "Yeah but I think you and the guys will like her. she has some great ideas for the place."

"Great."

"Have a seat. I'll bring your order out."

Turning around, I saw Zerrin and Josephine leaning in. They were chatting a little too close for my comfort. So, I headed quickly to the table.

. . .

My alarm loudly buzzed. I slapped it a couple of times before the incessant noise stopped. Flipping onto my back, I pushed the covers off and was sort of glad that particular dream ended. Damn Zerrin. Still, I missed Josephine and wished I could go back to my dream. I wanted to return to a time when Josphine was still alive and in my arms.

Without warning, a pounding headache pierce my head right behind my eyes. Struggling to get up, I wondered if the cause of the pain was the lack of part of my soul, but seriously I doubted that. Finally, I dragged myself out of the bed and trudged to the kitchen.

Jacob was sitting at the table. "What are you plans for today?" He asked while he dipped a spoon into a bowl of cereal.

Before I answered, I searched for some aspirin. Once I found a bottle, I popped two pills, swallowed them with a swig of water then sat down. "Not sure."

We need to go search for the other half of me.

But I wasn't going to tell Jacob that. So, I ignored Elvis.

"Will you be at the club later?"

"Maybe. Not sure. I think DB is a little perturbed with me right now."

"I don't think he can stay that way for long, can he?" Pushing his chair back, Jacob picked up his bowl and placed it into the sink.

"We can only hope."

Yes, we can.

After he left, I sat at the table for a few minutes contemplating what to do.

Are we going to sit here all day? Are we going to go search for my other half? Elvis prodded me.

I scoffed. "I guess we go in search of Selvis, but I have no idea where to start."

I think I know a place he could be hiding.
"Where?"
It's just a hunch, but worth a try.
"I'll try anything," I responded.
Good. Elvis's laughed reverberated in my head, causing me to need more aspirin. *We should get going.*
"Where are we going?"
1018 Royal Street.

Bridge

Baron Samedi

I TRAVELED through the Underworld determined to seek out what was causing the chaos down here. How dare someone do this without my permission, especially with my wife? The tunnels smelled of death and decay, a scent I relished. It was comforting, like a warm blanket.

The walls were filled with those I had imprisoned for one reason or another. Some, I had forgotten or did not really care to remember. Their skeletal arms and heads reached out to me, begging for me to free them from their prisons. I had no intention of doing as they wished. I had other business to attend to.

I decided to visit each one of the gates to see if the other loas might know who my dear wife may be working with.

My first stop was the sixth gate to see Baron Krimiel. He met me at his gate, his hands just barely resting on the wrought iron. The skeletons decorating the entrance chomped and bit at the loa, but he didn't dare let them get to him.

"Well, well what do I owe the honor of the great and powerful Baron Samedi to grace me at my gate?" He sneered and tipped his hat to me.

"Do not be rude," I warned, driving my staff into the soft dirt and taking a stand. "Let me in."

"Why should I?" He teased, leaning over the gate. Then he moved back, just before one of the little skeletons moved to attack.

"Because I need to speak to you about something happening down here."

Sucking in a deep breath, he opened his gate wide and bowed to me as I entered. "So, what is it that you need to speak to me about?"

A loud scream echoed all around us. It was so shrill it almost knocked both of us to the ground.

"What the hell was that?" I asked in shock.

Glancing around, my eyes landed on all tombs. They belonged to his plots that his grave digger had been digging, and they had collapsed inside the ground.

Find Out What's Happening
Rick

I stood across the street from 1018 Royal Street, staring at the red apartment building with the green shutters. Each balcony had a white, ornate iron fence. The place looked familiar and then it hit me. "Hey this is where you filmed part of King Creole?"

Yes, I sang Crawfish leaning over that balcony right up there.

"As many times as I've passed this building, it never fazed me. It never even crossed my mind that this was the building where you filmed a movie." I gasped in appreciation.

Yes. Now, let's get up to apartment number nine.

"Damn, I hope it's vacant," I muttered, climbing the stairs.

I hope so as well.

To our surprise, it was. Though the door was ajar, I knocked first before entering. Crossing the threshold, I was met with a surprised that shocked the hell out of me.

Sitting in the middle of the run-down apartment was none

other than the sofa from the Jungle Room. The Polynesian sofa, with its soft fuzzy cushions, stared back at me with the dragon-decorated armrests. They faux roared in protest of being in the dilapidated room and not their regular posh setup.

Off to the right, sat another. The wide cushy chair with an owl perched on the back void of its vintage teddy bear. "Is that what I think it is?" I gasped in shock.

It has to be. There can't be another like it. I mean who the hell would make two of these ugly pieces. Elvis laughed. It was comical because he had bought the pieces so long ago.

"Yeah but you bought this so called ugly furniture," I said. Walking through the room, I ran a hand over the intricate wood of the dragon heads. Damn, there was no way this is real. There was no way in hell I would ever be able to touch this furniture.

I wanted to sit down and feel the softness on my ass, but I didn't dare. Instead, I walked behind the sofa and noticed a pile of vinyl placed on the matching chair.

All right, Rick, go through those. There could be a clue.

"What makes you think that?"

I don't know, but since we know the furniture is from my home maybe those records came from there also.

Removing the albums, I dared to sit in their place. The cushion was the most comfortable thing I had ever felt. I practically melted into softness.

With the records on my lap, I started to flip through them. A slip of paper fluttered to the ground. Moving the LPs to the floor, I scooped it up.

Elvis hummed in my head as I glanced at the paper. It was a list of nine songs. It was some kind of set list.

Rick! Do you any of those songs spell out anything to you?" Elvis exclaimed loudly in my head, causing me to drop the paper

I shook my head. "No. Why should they?" Holding the side of my head, I leaned over and picked up the sheet with my other hand.

Okay humor me, he laughed as he read off just certain songs titles.

Mystery Train
Unchained melody
Never been to spain
If I can dream
Can't help falling in love
It's now or never
Playing for keeps
All shook up
Loving arms

"I don't see it." I was baffled.

So, I don't know if you know this but in nineteen fifty-six, I played at the Municipal Auditorium here in the city.

"Wait, the same one that resides beside the Mahlia Jackson theater?"

"Wait. You mean to tell me they named a theater after her? I could feel his smile inside my body. *Okay, but that wasn't there when I was around.*

"Yes, they did. Also, that auditorium is abandoned. Has been ever seen hurricane Katrina.

Then I say that Selvis is also hiding there. These songs are proof.

"How do you know?"

Because I feel it, Elvis revealed to me. *He's been living here, but I'm not sure what he's doing at the auditorium.*

"We need to find out what Selvis is doing there before someone else does."

Suddenly. a cold chill ran down my spine. It was as if someone was listening to our conversation. "Elvis, do you sense someone or something else here?" I asked, a little fearful of his answer.

No, but I did sense something earlier.

"Why didn't you say something?"

Because I thought maybe it was just the old apartment. Strange sensations are always evident in old places.

"Especially here in New Orleans. We are quite known for ghosts." *I whispered.*

I know that the bone man told me to be careful talking because he spies were among us.

"Pfft," I scoffed, already feeling ridiculous.

I decided to carefully walk through all the rooms before I left. Stopping in the bathroom, the sensation of someone being in the apartment was no more. I stared at my, or actually Elvis's, reflection in the mirror. It still amazed me that seventy's Elvis stared back at me. I shook my head yet the face staring back at me didn't go away.

Rick, let's get going to the Auditorium.

"You're right."

As I turned to leave, I took one last glance at the famous sofa and chairs. "I need to make sure your stuff is safe."

How do you plan to do that?

"Easy peasy." I pulled my cell from my pocket and texted the one person who would answer me even though he was upset with me.

Txt. *Pick up 1018 royal St Apt 9*
Left by Selvis
End txt

. . .

Few seconds a reply buzzed in

Txt. *What is it?*
    End txt

Txt. *You'll see*
    End txt

Txt. *Okay, be there in a few*
    End txt

Shutting the door behind me, I headed down the narrow steps. A chill in the air rolled through and wrapped around me. Shivering slightly, I pulled my jacket closer. For some odd reason, the street was empty, but I paid it no mind as I meandered down it to my destination.

Bridge Two
Baron Samedi

I looked at the grave digger in shock. His pants were covered in holes. He had been hard at work.

"What in the hell is going on here?" Making my way to him, I was careful not to fall inside the huge holes encompassing the entire area.

Raising his shoulders, the shovel hit the ground as he lifted his palms. "Samedi, I have no idea what's happening." Picking up the shovel, he leaned against a tomb that was still standing, holding it in his hand between his legs. "I've never witnessed anything like this in all my life. Which, as you know, has been awhile."

Glancing around, I wondered what in the world was happening. Turning to the gate keeper, I questioned, "Baron Kriminel, have you witnessed anything else out of the normal?"

"Besides this?" He waved a hand at the destruction.

I cocked a brow at him.

The skeletal man sauntered toward me. "Now, that you mention it, there have been whispers of souls missing or souls answering to someone else."

I tried to hold my fury at bay. "That's not possible. They answer only to me."

Leaning forward, he stopped mere inches from my face. "Are you sure, Samedi?"

Pushing back from him, I balanced on my staff. "Yes, Why would not I be?"

He shook his head. "We heard rumors that you are busy with your King of Rock and Roll and have let the souls lay to the side.

"Perhaps, but that does not mean someone else can come in and start controlling them," I angrily growled. "Have you seen this person?"

Kriminiel laughed. "No, it is all rumors, murmurs on the air, and in the waters of your precious Bayou of Lost Souls. Has your wife not said anything to you?"

No, she has not, which made me question things as well. But I was not going to say that out loud.

I looked back to the grave digger. "But what about this?" I waved a hand at the gaping holes.

Kriminel lifted his shoulders then dropped them in defeat. "I have no idea what in the hell this is, but I fear it has to do with an imbalance in the Underworld. There's something going on here."

I nodded. "You are right. I need to deal with this," I said, stabbing my staff into the dirt and disappearing to my office.

I Gotta Know
Rick

Walking down Royal Street, I came across a few tourists here or there. I paid it no mind. I had other things to think about.

Do you know where you are going? Elvis asked.

"Of course, I do."

Darkness shrouded the sky. No stars could be seen. The air took on an even chillier effect. The sudden darkness gave me an eerie feeling. Someone was following me.

I stopped, and looked off in the distance. Focusing my eyes, I saw nothing. Were my senses playing tricks on me?

Are you okay, Rick?

"Yes, I've just had this odd sensation that someone is following me. You know the old saying, 'someone walking over your grave'?"

Yes.

"Well, I've had that feeling ever since we left the apartment. I was trying not to let it bother me because I was on a mission."

I stopped suddenly at St Peters Street. Turning right, I continued. Crossing over Burgundy Street, I noticed a bar on the corner with a few dozen motorcycles parked at the curb.

I wonder what that place is? Elvis asked.

"We don't have time for that right now," I said, continuing down the street, then going up Rampart Street and crossing it.

The brilliant lit arches leading to Congo square called out, beckoning for all to come to its park. The tiny lights dazzled and illuminated the name Louis Armstrong

I hurried across the double lane road almost getting hit by a car. It swerved as not to cause an accident. Of course, the douchebag blew his horn at me and flipped me off as he drove away.

Making across unscathed, I looked up at the shining arches but before entering, I noticed someone. There was a muscular man straddling a motorcycle with both feet on the ground. His boots were firmly planted on the cement, keeping both man and motorcycle upright.

He looked rather familiar. Then, the hulking figure waved at me. I hesitantly walked to him.

"Can I help you?" I asked, vaguely placing how I knew him. Up close, he was even more massive.

"No, but I think I can help you." His smile was almost menacing, yet kind at the same time. He reached into his pocket. "Here, I think these belong to you." He handed me the keys the mugger had taken.

"Thank goodness. I was going to have to get the car dealership to order a new set. And since my car is vintage, it was going to cost me an arm and a leg."

"Good. Now, you don't have to worry about it."

"Thank you, how did you...?"

He waved my question off. "Just make sure Baron Samedi isn't doing you dirty."

I coughed sarcastically. I couldn't promise that. "Thanks for these." I tossed the keys from one hand to the other then nonchalantly shoved them in the back pocket of my jeans.

"Anytime. You ever need a drink come see me at the Stone Dragon." He motioned with his head toward Burgundy Street before starting his motorcycle and riding off.

How do you know that man? Elvis asked me as I continued under the arches.

"He's the one who helped me when I was injured.

And is this place safe?

"Yes, as long as we stay out of the shadows."

I chanced a glance over my shoulder as I kept walking. The motorcycle guy was still watching me from the entrance to Congo Square. I almost tripped over a rock because I wasn't paying attention.

Careful, Elvis chastised.

Quickly regaining my balance, I made my way through Congo Square.

Fourteen minutes from the time I left Royal Street, I stood staring up at the massive, abandoned Auditorium. It looked like something out of a haunted movie with its broken windows and graffiti decorating the exterior.

Wow, it sure has changed since I played here, Elvis exclaimed.

"Yeah a hurricane will do that." He ignored my comment.

Stealthily walking up to the doors, I tried to open them, but they didn't budge. The place was locked up tight.

If I remember, there was a back door. Maybe we can get in that way.

"Let's try."

Heading around the side, it was so quiet that I swore I heard the ticking of a clock. But that couldn't be. We were alone except for the boards, old fencing and two random dimpsty dumpsters.

The only movement was the occasional piece of trash that hadn't made its way into the trash receptacles blowing past. Just to make sure I was alone, I looked around, but saw nothing. There wasn't even the usual homeless person that should have taken up residence in this prime real estate.

"Let's go see if we can get inside."

Carefully making my way around the side of the building, I inched closer, looking over my shoulder every other step or so. I had to keep an eye out for anyone else in the vicinity. Once in front of the door, my nerves got the better of me and I stood there staring at the old metal door.

Come on, Rick. What's holding you back?

"What if we find him and he doesn't want to return with me?"

We'll cross that bridge when we come to it. Let's get this door open.

I pulled and pulled and pulled, but the door wouldn't budge. Nothing would make it move. Stepping back, I wiped the sweat from my brow with the back of my hand.

"Damn, it's not going to budge, just like the other one."

No, the other one was chained. This one is just stuck. Try again, Elvis pleaded.

Heaving a huge sigh, I wiped my hands on my jeans and tried again. This time the door opened slightly.

The dark sky grew darker. I swore I heard a low ticking sound on the other sound of the door. Putting my ear as close as possible to the door, the sound became muffled. I was determined. Pulling on the door, I managed to get it open just enough to squeeze through.

Upon walking inside, I noticed how huge it was. "You performed here?" I asked, very impressed.

I did.

I could feel his smile inside me which sort of tickled my senses. "What was it like?"

Once again before he spoke, I could feel his excitement ignite within my body.

It was the most exciting thing ever. And...uh the most...uh nerve wracking thing. I was so nervous at times. The crowds were enormous. And they... they were screaming for me. Which at times was exhilarating. He nervously laughed.

Walking over to the stage, I stepped up on it. There was a record player, the arm skipping over the record that had been left on the turntable. On further inspection, I noticed an unusual writing on the record. Pulling the arm off, the scratching immediately stopped. .

It can't be?

"Yes, it is." Robin's ghostly figure came from the back of the stage.

"What the hell are you doing here?" I asked.

"Waiting for Selvis to come back. Obviously, he got scared and well, he's not here," he muttered.

I turned my attention back to the record. "You were saying something about this." I removed it and held it in my hand.

Not actually a record but called an acetate. They can't be played as many times as vinyl.

Robin smiled. "Yes, Selvis said he snatched that. It is apparently the first acetate of That's All Right that Dewey Phillips played on the radio station in nineteen fifty-four." Robin's grin was wide.

All of a sudden, it felt like I was holding gold. I was afraid to drop it. My hands were suddenly sweaty. I thought at any moment, it would slide from my hand. I was afraid I would drop the precious commodity.

"What the hell do we do with this? I asked, wondering when the cops were going to find out about Selvis's thievery.

Robin's face fell flat.

"Oh, damn, I don't like that look."

What's wrong with his look? Elvis wondered in my head.

"You'll see. Follow me," Robin said, disappearing and reappearing in the back dressing room of the auditorium.

The only way I found him was to keep calling his name. Then, he would reappear in front of me.

Finally, when I was standing in the old, dilapidated dressing room, I understood his look. "What the hell is all of this?"

"This." He waved a hand at what I could only deduce was what the archives at Graceland looked like.

"So, what the hell do we do with all of this stuff?"

"I don't know, but I have already started taking the little things over to the club. I have been hiding them in a small alcove behind the dressing room. Selvis has me protecting it. In fact, he was going to give you something."

"Me?"

"Yes."

"What?"

"The starburst cape."

Ah, perfect choice.

"Why?"

For the scar on your neck.

My hand instantly went to touch the scar I never thought

about much. Inhaling deeply, I refocused. "Do you think he could be back at the club?"

"Anything's possible," Robin warned. "Why don't you go check there while I finish hiding all these items?"

As he said that, I heard a distant ticking of what sounded like a clock, but it disappeared just as quickly as I heard it.

Interlude

T had become a master at hiding in the shadows. This was no different. I snuck inside the old, dilapidated building. The second I shimmered inside, I was hit with a memory. One that contained my wife. I was taking her to see a concert.

Looking out into the sea of chairs crowded with people, I saw my wife. A smile etched on her face as she waited to see the king of rock and roll and his gyrating hips.

I never understood the allure of the man. His music was not to my taste, but it was pleasant to my wife. I preferred jazz with the sounds of the trumpet played by Louis Armstrong. It was more refined, not all this gyrating and shaking of one's body. Give me Dino, Ole Blue Eyes, Bobby Vinton, or even Nat King Cole.

The memory faded just as quickly as it had come and instantly, I missed her. My chest ached for her, but I pushed the pain down and away. I had a mission to complete so I would be able to see her again.

When I blinked through the haze, I noticed that this building was, of course, not how I remembered it. I pressed myself deep into a corner after following the tribute.

They were still outside trying to open the door. That feat was lost on me. I moved effortlessly in the shadows, so here I was staring at Selvis himself. He stood in front of the record player positioning the arm over the vinyl. I opened my pocket watch to check the time and watched as the half a soul that I was in search of picked up his head and in a flash–disappeared.

My chance to grab him was lost in those second, so, I just remained hidden as the one containing his other half made it inside. Paying close attention, I listened intently to what the live tribute and the dead tribute talked about. It was fascinating. Once they decided to leave, I knew what I had to do.

TRAVELING IN THE SHADOWS, I appeared below in the Underworld. Stalking through the tunnels, the stench of death was lost on me as skeletal arms reached out to me. They couldn't see me, so, I assumed they were just grabbing at anyone, begging to be let out of their prison.

Ignoring them, I glided, barely touching the dirty ground, and made my way to the Bayou of Lost Souls. Once there, I commanded my small pirogue to float through the throngs of lifeless souls. Some of them still begged for help from Baron Samedi to get to the seventh gate. I was not him and couldn't help them. So, I ignored their pleas for assistance and stepped onto my boat with ease.

The souls moved my pirogue, and it slowly, effortlessly moved through them. When I arrived at the island I called home, I hadn't planned on getting out, but something pulled at me. So, I stepped off the boat and blindly went deeply into the swamp where I lived. Hidden in a cypress tree was a box I held near a dear to me. but before I reached for my treasure, I turned on my radio to play one of *my favorite songs, Strangers in the Night.* As the melody lifted up through the branches and floated through the air I dug into the hole of the old cypress tree. Pulling out an old wooden box. I opened it up to reveal a pear-shaped garnet ring belonging to my wife. I missed her deeply and one day I would have her back in my arms. I scooped the ring out then as the last of the song played and ended, I sighed deeply putting the ring back in the box. One day my love, one day.

AFTER PLACING my treasure back where it belonged, I headed off to why I came out here. heading off to where the souls who were no more existed *I reached into the murky, stagnant water and grabbed one of them. He, she or it didn't fight, their wispy body just dangled in my hand.*

Chorus

Baron Samedi

I RETURNED to my office to find Erik and Skeley deep in conversation, Paying no attention to their drivel, I plopped down into my chair.

"What the hell is happening? Who the hell was commanding my souls?" I wondered aloud which got a reaction from the two in my office.

"What the hell are you talking about?" Erik's head spun on his shoulders.

Leaning on my desk, a feeling of defeat overcame me which saddened me.

"It appears someone, according to Kriminel, is commanding MY SOULS."

"But how is that possible?" Erik asked.

I shook my head. "That, I do not know."

"We must find out who this is," Skeley suggested.

"How do you plan we do this? We have not even found Selvis. Lawson is officially in hiding," I stated.

"I think it is that wife of yours," Skeley insisted.

I wanted to agree with him, but I didn't dare say it out loud.

A Mess of Blues
Rick

Walking into the dressing room, I was greeted by someone I'd hoped to see but never expected to see. He sat on my chair in front of the dressing table. Across his lap was the cape belonging to the Sunburst jumpsuit. His smile resembled the one of the soul living inside of me.

"It's nice to see you, Selvis," I welcomed.

Running a hand through his blond pompadour, he asked, "Were you expecting me?"

"I was hoping you'd be here."

"Why?" He suspiciously asked, crossing his legs, causing the cape to shift.

"Because we need to..."

He's not going to be that easy to catch and deliver to Baron Samedi, Elvis warned.

"Bring me back to Baron Samedi," Selvis laughed. "Why would you want to do that?"

"Shit, he can hear you?"

Sorry. Maybe if you tell him why you need to return him to Samedi, he'll go willingly, Elvis suggested.

"You know, you might be right," I agreed.

"Selvis, Baron Samedi enlisted me to return you to him."

The half a soul rubbed the material of the cape, then looked up at me. "Why?"

"He knows you and Elvis need to be put back together soon."

Before I could react, something or someone came out of the shadows and grabbed Selvis, leaving the Cape floating to the floor. Shocked, I stood staring as Robin suddenly appeared out of nowhere.

"What the hell happened?" He asked.

"I have no clue, but I do know one thing."

"What's that?" Robin asked shaking his head.

"I'm going to have to explain to the bone man that I wasn't able to contain Selvis."

Shit! The bone man is going to be pissed, Elvis agreed.

I didn't need to hear that, but sadly, I concurred.

"There's one other thing to discuss." Robin leaned against the mirrors.

"What is it?" Elvis and I asked in unison.

"Come see. Remember, I told you I was bringing stuff here from the Auditorium.

"Yes. What is it?" I nodded my head apprehensively Shit."

"You won't believe it unless I show it to you."

Ushering us into the back of the dressing room, we entered a section I'd never before seen. An array of items sat haphazardly, left where they been placed. It looked like a shrine to the person inhabiting my body.

"What is this?"

I don't know," the ghostly Robin stated as he walked through the items.

"I think I do," I thought aloud. "He's desperately trying to get back together with Elvis."

I guess now you are the keeper of all my stuff, Robin, Elvis observed.

"Yeah, until we find Selvis." Robin's eyes roamed the room. "I wonder where he went, or for that matter, who grabbed him. Let's face it, that was the most unusual way of leaving." Robin tossed one of the items back and forth in his hands.

"You're right," I agreed. "It was creepy."

Interlude

Entering the club with a piece of a soul shoved into my pocket watch, I had a plan. What I found fascinating was Selvis, and they just happened to be talking with him.

The conversation continued, and I remained quiet. I found out information that my benefactor would love to know. It became apparent that the big man wanted two souls but my benefactor could use the one. Stepping out of the shadows without anyone seeing me, I snatched the blond one.

With my full proof way to keep Selvis inside the pocket watch, there was another surprise the Underworld for which no one was prepared. I didn't want Selvis to get out again, so, I removed the watch from my pocket and with a careful touch squeezed Selvis inside the other soul. He squealed in protest but it didn't help his situation.

It nestled alongside him, disgruntling the other half of the King of Rock and Roll. He didn't look bit happy at all, but I knew who would be happy, Maman Bridgitte.

How can you Lose What You Never Had
Rick

August 16th

I had to bite the bullet so to speak and tell the bone man I had failed to retrieve Selvis for him. To make matters worse, I had no idea who took him.

After finding Selvis' stash at both the Municipal Auditorium and the dressing room, I knew Robin was the man to keep the items safe. I sat at the bar with the cape wrapped around my shoulders.

"It looks good on you." DB came up from behind me. Nodding without looking at him, I just sat there with the glass of bourbon and watched the ice melt.

"Where did you get it? I know you have the jumpsuit but when did you get the cape?" he said walking up and inspecting me. he gasped as he sat beside me. "Is that what I think it is?"

I nodded and didn't say a word.

I think my other half picked a good item to leave you.

"Thanks," I said, nursing a drink, twirling the glass on the bar.

"Robin tells me someone or something took Selvis before you could convince him to go back to the Underworld with you."

I nodded.

"Shit! what the hell? What are we going to do?"

"Nothing to do." I took a sip of bourbon. "I have to pay the pied piper so to speak."

"That's very brave of you."

I hung my head. "What do I have to lose or what choice do I have? I can't run. This is my life, or death, so to speak.

At that moment, a loud crack boomed around us. The bone man appeared. He didn't look well–almost as if he was going through his own drama.

"Rick, do you have Selvis?"

I turned on the bar stool. "I need to confess."

His eyes turned black and for a split second, I thought about running. Sadly, I didn't know how far I would get. So, I remained on my barstool, glass in hand, and drank my bourbon.

Leaning against the bar, his staff in his hand, the skeletons on the Baron's stiff clacked at each other. "Where is Selvis then?"

"Someone, someone invisible, snuck in while I was trying to convince him to return to you, and grabbed him."

"Son of a bitch!" His roar shook the walls. Pictures fell. Glass shattered. Even the glasses behind the bar exploded.

His eyes turned from black to red, and fear shot through me. Then, in the blink of an eye, he managed to calm down.

"Since you failed, I guess I get to dole out your punishment."

"I guess so."

Pulling an envelope from his pocket, he scoffed, "Here this is yours. Read."

He handed me the letter from Josephine. I didn't see how reading a letter from the love of my life was a punishment, but I soon would.

Opening it, I began to read.

DEAR RICK,

I KNOW after reading this letter you will be devastated, but honestly, I don't know any other way to break the news to you. I fell in love with someone else while stationed in Germany. He is a kind soul and much like you.

I STOPPED READING. I couldn't believe it. Who could it have been. Then as memories played over and over in my head only one person popped into my head. There was no way ex-my best friend betrayed me, not once, but twice. Looking at DB and the others, I fought back my anger mixed with tears and continued reading.

WHEN HE CAME TO VISIT, I ended up pregnant. We didn't know how to tell you since you two were no longer speaking. So, I decided to send you a letter. I'm very sorry. Just know that I did love you.

. . .

Yours truly,
   Josephine.

Without a word, I finished, then tore it into a dozen pieces. No one said a word as I sat there in silence contemplating the betrayal from my girlfriend and ex-best friend.

It didn't matter that Zerrin hadn't been my friend for a long time, it was betrayal–plain and simple. Suddenly, I jumped from the barstool, causing it to spin.

"I need some air."

"Rick, don't do anything stupid," Robin pleaded as he followed.

"Wait! Where the hell is he going?" The skeletal man asked my retreating figure. "I need to take Elvis back to the Underworld.

"Let him go. He'll be back," DB told him as I practically pulled the door off the hinges leaving the club.

Where are you going? Elvis asked, but I ignored him.

I'd never been angrier in my life. How could Zerrin and Josphine do this to me?

As the question came to mind, I found myself behind the wheel of my car. Turning the key, the engine roared to life and I pulled away from the curb. I had every intention of making my way over the causeway bridge.

Where are you going?

"To confront the asshole who ruined my world," I growled through gritted teeth.

Do you think that will soothe your broken heart? Elvis knowingly inquired. *Besides how do you know it was him. His name wasn't mentioned in the letter.*

"No, but I'm certain it will make me feel better when I knock his ass out," I snarled, amping up my speed.

The rest of the trip was done in silence as I contemplated what to do or say to Zerrin.

TWENTY-FIVE MILES later

I ENDED up sitting in my car, staring at the blinking sign that read the Flaming Star.

How long are you going to sit here?

"Don't know," I snapped, then slid from the car.

Are you sure you want to do this?

"Yes, I do," I growled, storming into the club.

The song *Mean Woman Blues* blared through the club and the lack of bodies inside didn't muffle the sound. The lights were low. I could see a few people scattered about. Closer to the stage sat Lain Crew and Austin Avery plus a few other tributes I didn't recognize.

Zerrin was on stage moving like Elvis. He clapped his hands to the rhythm of the song, but the few measly stragglers never even looked up from their drinks.

Damn, he moves just like me.

"Yes, but we aren't here to appreciate his moves." I retorted angrily. I walked down the aisle on a mission.

What are we here for then?

"To settle a score," I snapped, stopping just short of the stage.

"Stop, stop. Zerrin stopped the music in the middle of the song with a wave of his hand to the band and stared at me. "Rick what are you doing here?"

"As if you don't know." I grumbled irritably.

Ignoring his apology, I started to ascend the steps.

Kingston ran up to me. "Rick, what are you doing here?" He put a hand on my shoulder to pull me back, but I shrugged it off.

Don't do this. Elvis pleaded.

I ignored him, letting my rage take over.

"I have no idea why you're here." Zerrin tried to calm me down.

"You shouldn't be here." Kingston tried to pull at me again.

"You're damn right!" I seethed. "But Zerrin has betrayed me." Continuing toward Zerrin without hesitation, I landed a haymaker to his face. He hit the ground. I shook my hand as he wiped blood from his nose and looked up at me.

Do you feel better? Elvis asked.

I didn't answer him. I just stared down at Zerrin, wishing he hadn't betrayed me.

"What the hell was that for?" Kingston rushed to Zerrin's side, looking at me for an answer.

"He knows why," I spat, stalking off the stage and through the club, and letting the door slam.

Did that childish behavior make you feel better? Elvis lectured as I made my way back to the car.

"As a matter of fact, I do feel somewhat better," I replied, sighing and rubbing my knuckles.

Now, where are you going?

Shrugging, I sighed, "I don't know, but I need to get away from here."

Sliding behind the wheel, I started to drive and ended up back over the causeway. The sky above me was pitch dark, except for the stars twinkling high overhead, but they didn't matter.

I couldn't see the guardrails on either side of me. If a car hit me, I could go over, and no one would ever know. Twenty-five miles later, I was back on the other side. I drove until I ended up by the lake.

Stopping the car, I just sat there for a while, watching the water lap against the seawall. Gripping the steering wheel, I couldn't believe all that had happened to get me where I was.

Rick, what are we doing here? Shouldn't we go back to the club?

Ignoring Elvis, I sighed deeply. Opening the door, I got out. The cool breeze swept across my face as I got closer to the water. The lake breeze floating through the air smelled of salt and the scent of fish.

The urge to think surpassed all else that played in my mind, so I found a bench overlooking the water. I couldn't believe that my best friend and the love of my life had an affair.

A memory flooded into my subconscious like the waves hitting against the seawall.

"Come on, Josephine. Just one song," I prodded.

She blushed as I stood in the club with microphone in hand.

"I can't." *She sat at the table right in the front of the stage.*

Zerrin came over and sat beside her. He smiled. It struck me as odd, but I dismissed it as him being friendly.

I nodded to him to turn the karaoke machine on and the song Wearing That Loved On Look *started to play. Putting the mic to my mouth, I belted out the words. Moving my hips to the beat of the song, the others in the club sang along as did Josephine.*

Smiling, I jumped off the stage and held the mic to her lips. She joined in, singing the words with me. We had the whole club singing and dancing.

At the end, I bent down and planted a kiss on her lips. It was like magic. It sent my world spinning out of control.

Return to Sender
Baron Samedi

I could not believe this was happening. How could he just have walked out with my King of Rock and Roll?

"Here sir, why don't you have a drink?" Bri slid a glass my way as I watched Betty speaking to Robin in the corner of the bar.

Taking the drink, I was about to sit when DB returned. "Any word?"

"Not yet." I glanced at my wrist. "It's almost midnight."

Waving a gloved hand, a shimmery scene appeared on the stage. We had arrived just in time to witness Rick cold cock a guy in the face.

"Why would he do that?" I looked at DB for answers.

Chuckling, he looked down at the tiny pieces of torn paper littering the floor. "I'm guessing it has to do with the letter you gave him."

I threw my head back. "Ah, that was actually a great read."

"You knew what was in the letter before you gave it to him?" He was shocked.

"Of course, why do you think I gave it to him?" I smiled eerily.

"That's mean."

I nodded. "Of course, it is, and quite funny. But I didn't know it was an old friend she mentioned in the letter." Watching the hazy scene play out, the thud of a glass on the wooden bar sounded. Quickly turning, I witnessed Bri passing me another rum. "Thanks."

"My pleasure, sir." She smiled and started wiping down the bar.

Spinning on the barstool, I crossed my legs and watched Rick, wondering where he was going. I checked my watch one last time. At the thirty-minute mark, I knew I had to go to him. He was not coming back.

Mind made up, I finished the rum and slammed the glass on the bar, smiling at my skeletons on my staff. "Are you guys ready?" They clacked in response.

Without telling anyone goodbye, I stabbed my staff seven times and disappeared in a puff of smoke.

Appearing beside Rick on the wooden bench, I asked, "Are you ready to let go of your companion?"

Screaming loudly in fright, he turned around, grasping his heart. "Jesus! You scared this shit out of me!"

Chuckling low, I leaned against the bench. "Well, I figured you weren't coming back to the club, so, I came to you. Elvis must be taken out of you."

You know you will be okay, Elvis comforted.

"I doubt that. I mean, I have half a soul that I lost for a

woman who didn't truly love me." Inhaling deeply, I looked out over the water and it seemed to do the trick.

"Let's get ready for this. I have things to handle in the Underworld," Baron Samedi declared, stabbing his staff into the ground.

Keeping my attention on the waves as they crested against the seawall, I asked the skeletal man, "Once this is done, how am I going to survive with half my soul?"

Baron Samedi shrugged. "We will have to see. Now, let's get that King of Rock and Roll out of you." This time when he stabbed the ground with his staff again, it was infinitely more defiant.

It took only a few seconds for the beautiful loa of the sea to appear in all her glory. Rising straight from the water she was like something from a movie. Her long black hair shone under the moonlight, glistening as water droplets clung to it and every inch of her body.

Walking toward us, her iridescent legs caught my attention. It was the most amazing thing. Watching them turn from tail to legs, made me forget all my problems for a minute.

"Samedi, you called?"

"Yes, Sirene. It's so nice to see you again. We need to remove the King of Rock and Roll from this human."

She looked at me. "Hmm." Peering closer, she looked back to the skeletal man. "I must take precautions with this one."

"Why?" The words flew from my mouth as panic filled every fiber of my being.

Turning back to me, she placed a cold hand on my shoulder. "I need to make sure to remove the correct half soul.

Morpheus knew

Every dream has a price
He kisses your ear
As he hands you the dice ♫

HER HAND REMAINED on my shoulder, and her gaze remained intense as she sang the song backwards.

Morpheus comes
To peddle his rhyme
To those who'll sign
On the dotted line

To walk upon the earth again
To feel the wind on stolen skin
For just one glimpse of light
Free from their eternal night

Morpheus walks
On a path of bones
Of those who gambled
And sold their souls

♪ *Morpheus comes*

And peddles his dreams
Quilts of mist
With golden seams

UNLIKE WHEN ELVIS was put inside, it felt like my insides were being pulled from me as he was removed. I was going to have to ask Aaron and Robin if they felt such intense pain or if it was because I was missing half of my soul.

Soon, Elvis was sitting beside me on the bench.

"It's nice to see you again, outside of my body. Though, I'm not sure how I'm going to survive without you."

"You will do just fine without me. How are you feeling? How's your neck?"

My hand went to the scar. It felt almost nonexistence.

"We must be going now. I have to get him back to Guede Nibo's. We've wasted enough time here topside."

"I must be leaving as well," Sirene said.

"Thank you for your help, Sirene."

"It was my pleasure. I love helping you out and seeing the handsome creature." She smiled at Elvis as if she wanted to devour him like the humans did. Not even she was immune to his spell.

The three of us watched her sashay back into the lake. Diving into the water, her beautiful legs once again turned into a beautiful green and blue tail.

"We must be heading back as well. Tell DB I'll talk to him soon."

"Wait! What about me?" Rick asked.

"What about you?" I looked over my shoulder before leaving, my staff in hand, and the other on Elvis's shoulder.

"What's going to happen to me with half a soul?"

I laughed loudly. "Well, we'll just have to find out, now, won't we? But don't worry, your other half is safe and sound. I promise."

With that, I stabbed my staff into the ground and disappeared.

Bringin It Back
Rick

S itting alone on the bench, a sense of dread enveloped me. What the hell was I to do? A smile crept across my face as I stood, knowing perfectly well what I was going to do—I was going home.

Thirty minutes later, I walked inside to see Jacob and Aaron sitting on the sofa in our apartment, watching TV. As I tossed my keys on the table by the door, a news broadcaster came on with an urgent report.

"This is a breaking story from WWL. We have a breaking news story. We are reporting from Graceland in Memphis Tennessee." The reporter smiled at the camera.

"It appears that the famous Jungle Room where Elvis Presley recorded such hits as *Moody Blues* has been broken in to." The reporter walked inside the famed house as others, including security guards, stood watch around the house. "We have been allowed an exclusive inside look," she explained as she entered with her camera man.

As the newscaster reported Jacob and Aaron gasped. I didn't. I knew who had stolen the furniture.

Turning to me, their mouths opened wide in an accusatory fashion as they asked in unison. "Why do you not seem shocked?"

"Because I'm not. I've seen it and I know who stole it."

More gasped as they once again spoke in unison. "Who stole it?"

"Selvis."

"But I don't have time to explain any more. I need to get to the club and speak to DB. I have to make sure he's hidden the pieces well."

They just stared. As I grabbed my keys, they stopped me by saying, "We need to go with you unless the cops are on their way here."

I laughed. "I doubt they are. They have no idea how the furniture got out of there."

"Speaking of, How the hell *did* Selvis get that furniture out? Damn, Elvis had to practically take the back part of his house off to get it in when he bought it. So, I gotta ask again, how in the hell did Selvis get it out of Graceland?" Aaron was flummoxed.

"I'm thinking, because he's a soul, he probably enlisted other souls to help. That's all I can think of..."

And just like that, I was struck with a headache. Rubbing my temples with the tips of my fingers, I tried to think of an answer to the burning question, but came up empty handed.

Finally, I shook my head. "You know what Aaron, who the hell really knows? Perhaps the damn skeletal man is playing with us and this whole time he helped him steal it." It was the only explanation that made sense. With my hand on the doorknob, I added, "All right, if we are going to go, let's go."

FIFTEEN MINUTES later

THE THREE OF US walked into the club. "Hey, DB where are you?" I called the boss man.

It took a few minutes, but he finally walked into the club. "What's up guys?"

"Oh, nothing really, but have you seen the news?" I said, looking around for Betty or even Bri. When I didn't see them, I stepped behind the bar and grabbed a bottle of bourbon.

Nodding, he huffed, "I have and I'm busy taking care of it." Glaring at me, he continued, "I see you are still missing have your soul."

I didn't appreciate his tone, but I needed to think. Pouring some bourbon into a glass, I finally looked at him. "Well, if you can figure out a way for me to get it back, I'm all ears." I didn't even try to keep the sarcasm out of my tone. "Who knew the love of my life would betray me with my best friend, get pregnant, and then die? I guess that's what they mean by hindsight is twenty/twenty, right?" Not waiting for an answer, I threw back the bourbon I had just poured.

The door to the club opened and in walked Zerrin. "What the hell is he doing here?" I mumbled slamming down a glass.

"Please don't hit him. I heard what you did at Kingston's place." He leaned toward me. "Hear him out I don't think he was the one mentioned in the letter." DB told me before walking off and leaving us alone.

Zerrin walked up to the bar nursing a broken nose and sporting a black eye. "Did you come back for more?" I sneered.

"No but I'd like to know what's your problem with me? It can't possibly be competition." He looked around. "Because y'all seem to be doing way better than we are.

"One word Josephine."

He scoffed. "I haven't seen her in months."

I glared at him. "Are you sure because I got a letter from her saying otherwise."

He slid up onto the barstool and looked at me. "Rick did the letter actually have my name in it." he cocked his head at me.

I hung my head in shame. "No it didn't."

"Well then why are you assuming it was me she was talking about then."

"But you were at her funeral."

He signed deeply. "Because we used to be friends and I was," he stopped and looked around," I was worried about you. I knew how much you cared about her. I hated what happened with DB and Kingston and how it tore all of us apart."

Before he finished, the door to the club swung open, the handle hitting the wall behind it, and a slim woman stalked in like she owned the place. "Hey! Are ya'll open?" She asked.

"We are not, but come in anyway," DB kindly said. "How can I help you?"

"Hi! I'm Abigail. I work over at the Blue Moon Gallery."

"Ah, yes. You're Summer's new assistant."

She smiled. "Yes. She sent me over here. She wants to know how much longer you will be keeping that furniture in the gallery?"

DB sighed. "Tell her not much longer. Just trying to get in touch with someone who can move it back where it belongs."

"Good, because she's sort of freaking out," she said, sitting down at the bar.

"Would you like a drink?" I asked, starting to pour one.

"By the way, did yall know there is a skeleton living in the gallery?"

We stared at her. I stopped mid-pour.

"You can see Hyla?"

"Is that her name?"

"Yes, it is," Aaron said.

"Is she harmless?"

Aaron laughed. "Yes, she definitely is. As long as you leave her alone to do her art."

Abigail nodded her head. "Good, because she really is a great artist."

"Yes, she did all the stuff in here." DB motioned to the artwork on the walls.

"Wait! How can you see her?"

I knew there was a trick to seeing the dead since most of us could only see them, minus Jacob at this point.

She shrugged. "Not sure really. I know my mom always said I had a sixth sense about these things." Taking the drink, I offered her, she turned to DB. Scribbling her number on a piece of paper, she offered, "Let me know when you can get the furniture out. The gallery will be closed until then. You know, so no one finds out." She winked at him then left.

Coda
Baron Samedi

Dan pressed his body against the wall, not looking at me, but I could tell he was not happy. That was not really my problem. He was busy watching the tributes as they performed on stage.

I couldn't keep my eyes off them either. However, the one missing, the one with half a soul, I honestly hadn't expected to be up there. I was sure he was in mourning.

I almost dared not to ask where he was, but, being the loa of the dead, what was really stopping me. "Where is Mr. Miceli?" I asked in an almost singsong voice as I balanced on my staff, the skulls dancing to and fro to the beat of the music from the stage.

Before Dan turned to face me, he took a deep breath, biding his time to find the right words before he answered. Being a patient loa, I waited.

Deciding he was never going to say a single word, he finally answered. His tone was curt and he didn't look at me, but his anger flowed from every word he spoke. "Baron Samedi, his whereabouts are none of your business."

"Why are you getting testy with me?" I grumbled.

Ignoring me, he continued, "I will only say this once, you will give Rick back the half of his soul that you stole."

I gasped, placing a hand against my heart in feigned hurt. "I did not steal it from him. I gained it fair and square, and you had better watch who you speak to in that tone."

That's when he turned to glare at me. His expression was one I had only seen once. "I've done quite a bit for you, so you can do one thing I ask of you."

Holding back my own anger, the skulls on my staff grew quiet at my behest as I squeezed the stick. "Do you know who you are speaking to like that?"

He nodded, but didn't say a word, just remained standing against the wall in one of his many shiny jackets. Chancing a quick glance at me, his blue eyes twinkled with a hint of blackness. I loved that about him.

"Fine, but you know I will need a sacrifice in exchange for his soul."

Sighing, his chest heaved. I knew what he was thinking, so, I added, "You must give me something that you love as much as you love those boys."

He sighed again. "You will get what you desire, Baron Samedi. Now leave.

As I went to tap the floor with my staff, he stopped me. Still not looking at me, he declared, "But I would like Rick's soul returned tonight."

I growled, not entirely liking the way he spoke to me. Hitting my staff on the floor with such force that wood chips flew around me, I disappeared in a puff of smoke. As I flashed out of his sight, I heard his screams echo around me. "Damn it, Baron Samedi, not the fucking wood floor!"

STANDING outside my office I sucked in a deep breath before entering. The problem with this scenario was I was not sure I could put the soul back together.

The first time I did this, it was an accident and that soul had been separated for a while now. This time, I did it on purpose.

Walking into my office, I saw Erik sitting there. "Ahh. just the person I need to ask for a favor."

"Uh oh, it doesn't sound good," Skeley laughed from his painting on the wall.

Erik rolled his eyes and stuffed his phone back into the pocket of his pants. "What do you need from me?" He grimaced.

"Don't give me that look Erik. It shouldn't take too long. I need you to go to the witch's house and ask her for a spell."

"What type of spell?"

I sighed. wishing I did not have to go into detail with the peons.

"Wait! What soul? I thought you didn't get Selvis," Erik squealed like a stuck pig.

"Damn, Erik! Just do as I ask." Slumping into my chair, I was exhausted.

"Fine," he harrumphed, exiting my office with a slam of the door.

"Do you feel like talking about what's bothering you? Skeley asked, leaning against the oak tree in his painting, his skeletal arms resting behind his head.

"No, I do not, not tonight, Skeley."

"I'll be here all night if you change your mind," he said, sliding down and plopping himself in front of the tree. Picking up one of the books lying in the grass beside him, he started to read.

Twenty minutes later

Erik entered with a swing of the door, but he did not look happy. He held one of his arms under the other one.

"Geezus, what the hell happened to you?" Skeley asked, dropping his book onto the grass and trying to stifle his laughter.

Erik didn't answer the painting, just dropped a slip of paper onto my desk. "Here's your spell," he angrily grumbled. "She also told me that there might be a chance things will not be as they once were." Falling into the chair, he struggled to pop his arm back into place.

Walking around the desk, I grabbed the slip of paper. Opening it, I turned to him with a smirk. It was then that I noticed bite marks on his arm. "Let me guess, Rosie's dog got a hold of your arm.

He eyed me with disdain. "Yes, she thought I was a chew toy."

"Oh, no, she didn't," Skeley finally let out the burst of laughter I knew he had been holding onto.

"Stop it. Skeley," I ordered, approaching him to get the rum bottle from the safe. "Cover your ears, Erik."

Erik held his ears, though it was rather hard with one arm.

As I opened the safe a devilish idea popped into my head. Another bottle sat nestled inside. "Hmm you know I never actually agreed on which half of a soul I would return now did I?" Smirking I removed the vintage bottle. "Hello ole friend." I peered into the dark amber bottle barely able to see the soul who crossed his arms glaring at me from inside the bottle.

"Who is that?" Erik asked from my desk.

I turned and raised it. "A dear friend of mine who used to sing Elvis as well, Mr. Rick Perkins. Once I had the rum bottle in hand and the slip of paper, I disappeared to go topside. Reappearing inside the dark club, Rick sat at the bar.

To be continued in:

VK THE DEAD CREOLE CLUB

OTHER BOOKS BY THE AUTHOR

Voodoo Vows Series

The Alchemist Prophecy A Prequel

Magical Memories A Voodoo Vows Short Story

Voodoo Vows

Ghosts from the Past

Black Magic Betrayal

Spellbound Sacrifice

Ghosts from the Present

Devine Descent

The Guardians A Voodoo Vows Tail

Bred by Magic

Gifted by Magic

Mystical Mansion Series

Mystical Mortality

The Clover Chronicles

Finding a Leprechaun

Bayou Kiss Series

Summer's Kiss

Stand Alone

An Unexpected Hero

The Dead Creole Club

DB King The Dead Creole Club

Aaron Jesse The Dead Creole Club

Robin Davis The Dead Creole Club

∼

WRITTEN BY GENEVIEVE LAFLEUR

The Vieux Carre MC

The Gryphon's Revenge

Crescent Sentries

Stone Hearts

The Brotherhood of Redemption

The Protector's Kiss

COMING SOON

Voodoo Vows

Charmed Covenant

Ghosts from the Future

Mystical Mansion Series

Mystical Mansion

Mystical Mayhem

The Dead Creole Series

VK The Dead Creole Club

Blood Stone and Shadow Sorcery

Death of a Marauder

About the Author

Diana Marie DuBois resides in the historical and richly cultured-filled state of Louisiana just outside of the infamous city of New Orleans. She shares her home with one beautiful Great Dane. As a young girl Diana was an avid reader and could be found in her public library. Now you find her working in her local library, where she reads anything and everything. She has many story ideas with plenty of interesting characters running through her head.

ABOUT THE ELVIS TRIBUTE ARTIST

Nick Perkins, a multi-award-winning Elvis Tribute Artist, has been paying tribute to Elvis Presley since the age of sixteen. His unwavering passion for Elvis and his music radiates through every performance, each one delivered with the utmost respect for the man he believes is the greatest entertainer of all time.

Among his many accomplishments, Nick won the renowned Tupelo Elvis Festival and secured a spot in the Top 5 at Graceland's Ultimate Elvis Tribute Artist Contest, further cementing his reputation as one of the top tribute artists in the industry.

In addition to his tribute performances, Nick has broadened his career by founding Perkins Entertainment.

Made in the USA
Columbia, SC
08 June 2025